Joseph doesn't want his privileged classmates at the Academy to know he's a scholarship student from a working-class family. Or that his parents are immigrants. And he certainly doesn't want them to know he's a Unionist—not when they all hope that Maryland will secede and join the Confederacy.

Now the first troops from the north are passing through Baltimore, and Joseph is eager for a glimpse of the men who were so quick to answer Lincoln's call to put down the southern states' rebellion. But thanks to a chance meeting, his classmate Harold is beside him, waiting to taunt and jeer at "Lincoln's hirelings."

When the first of the northern troops march past, Joseph feels a swell of pride and patriotism he doesn't dare show. But his pride quickly changes to concern—and then to fear—as the unruly crowd becomes a howling mob.

JOSEPH SCHWARTZ'S STORY

JOSEPH SCHWARTZ'S STORY

Carolyn Reeder

A Children's Literature Paperback

First Children's Literature Printing: October, 2007
Originally published by HarperCollins: January 2003
as a novella in the hardback *Before the Creeks Ran Red*,
Library of Congress Control Number 2002023841.

Cover Image: Library of Congress, Prints & Photographs Division, LC-USZC4-
1736.

ISBN 978-1-890920-16-6
Printed in the U.S.A.

10 9 8 7 6 5 4 3 2 1

THE *BEFORE THE CREEKS RAN RED* TRILOGY

First published in hardback as a trio of linked novellas, the stories of Timothy Donovan in Charleston Harbor, Joseph Schwartz in Baltimore, and Gregory Howard in Alexandria, Virginia, are being reissued separately as a paperback trilogy. Though the ending of each story sets the stage for the next, they can be read in any order.

Timothy Donovan's Story. Timothy is a fourteen-year-old orphan and a bugler with the U.S. Army. At Fort Sumter, he faces the threat of bombardment by secessionist forces – and the continuing taunts of a soldier who sees him as good for nothing but sounding bugle calls.

Joseph Schwartz's Story. Joseph, also fourteen, is a working-class Baltimore boy with a scholarship to a private academy. As he struggles to hide his Unionist convictions and his family's circumstances from his rich, Confederate-leaning classmates without actually lying, he is caught up in a riot that breaks out as northern soldiers answering Lincoln's call for troops march through the city.

Gregory Howard's Story. The son of a privileged family in Alexandria, thirteen-year-old Gregory's life changes for the worse when Virginia votes for secession. It's bad enough that his father sides with the Union while the rest of the family supports the Confederacy. But then undisciplined Union troops occupy the city and harass the citizens, and Gregory finds himself facing a whole new set of problems.

A NOTE TO THE READER

The German spelling of the name Joseph is *Josef*, but I have written it as *Yosef*—the way his family pronounced it.

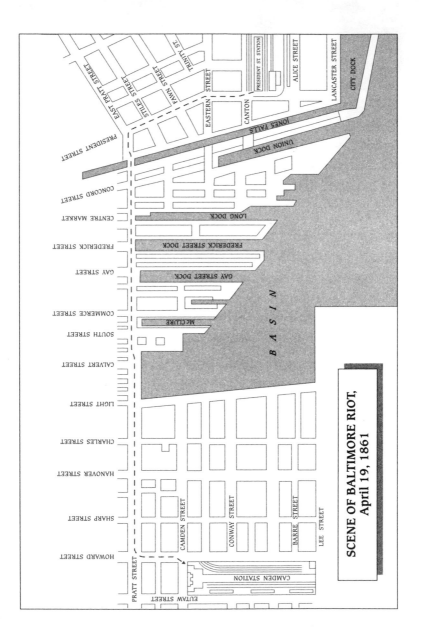

SCENE OF BALTIMORE RIOT,
April 19, 1861

CHAPTER ONE

"**H**EY, JOSEPH—we're going to the sweet shop. Want to come?"

Surprised to be invited, Joseph hesitated a moment before he said, "Thanks anyway, Harold, but I'd better get on home." He could hold his own in the classroom or in the school yard, but anywhere else he felt like a fish out of water. What did a scholarship student from the working-class neighborhood near the harbor have in common with boys whose families lived in fine houses and had slaves to wait on them?

Alexander, the one classmate Joseph didn't like, sneered and said, "What's the matter, Joe? Can't afford a penny candy?"

Bristling, Joseph reached in his pocket and pulled out the coins Ma had given him that morning. "I can afford to buy anything I want," he lied. "I could even treat you and Harold."

"Then what are we waiting for? Come on, Joe."

Joseph slung his book strap over his shoulder and followed his classmates out the door and down the hall. Now he'd really gotten himself in a pickle. He was supposed to stop at the butcher shop to buy sausage for supper, and Ma would kill him if he came home empty-handed.

Outside, the April sunshine was bright and the trees were leafing out, but it was the boy hawking newspapers on the corner who captured everyone's attention. "Extra! Extra! Virginia votes for secession! Read all about it," the newsboy called. "Virginia to join Confederacy!"

Harold and Alexander cheered enthusiastically, and Joseph tried to hide his dismay. "That must be the reason for the hundred-gun salute we heard during geography class," he said, figuring that was a safe enough reaction.

His eyes bright with excitement, Alexander declared, "It's about time Virginia left the Union—they waited long enough."

Harold nodded. "Maryland's waited too long. We should secede and join the Confederacy, too."

"And the sooner the better," Alexander said. "Don't you agree, Joe?"

Joseph's heart sank. Until the bombardment of Fort Sumter less than a week before, everyone had hoped the confrontation between North and South would be settled peacefully. But once rebel shots were fired, Lincoln had called on the loyal states to send volunteers to put down the insurrection. And now Joseph's classmates—along with so many others in the city—clamored for Maryland to join the seceded states rather than fight against them. "I think we'd be better off if Maryland stays neutral," he hedged, unwilling to admit he was a Unionist.

"Fat chance of that, when you see Confederate flags just about everywhere you look. If you ask me—" Alexander broke off at the sound of running feet.

Joseph looked behind them and saw a boy zigzagging between the pedestrians on the sidewalk, two men practically on his heels. *Must be a pickpocket.* The man in the lead was catching up, and Joseph waited for him to clamp a hand on the young pickpocket's shoulder. His eyes widened when the man drew even with the boy and then passed him.

Men and a few older boys were running along the other side of the street, too. "Come on," one of them yelled. "We've got to stop them!"

"Let's see what's going on," Joseph said. If they were running, he wouldn't have to answer Alexander's questions—or spend Ma's money at the sweet shop.

Crossing the street, he was jostled by a couple of rough-looking youths hurrying past, and on the sidewalk again he edged around several well-dressed men who had stepped out of a building. Near Howard Street, he became aware of a dull, roaring sound—a sound like rushing water, or maybe a windstorm. Where had he heard that before? *At Monument Square, when the people were heckling a speaker.* It was the sound of a crowd. An angry crowd.

Joseph was breathing hard by the time he saw the wall of people ahead of him. He stopped at the edge of the noisy, shoving mass and asked an older boy, "What's going on?"

"Baltimore's been invaded, that's what," the boy said,

and then he yelled, "Death to the northern oppressors!"

Harold and Alexander ran up in time to hear a scholarly-looking man explain, "The first of the three-month volunteers answering Lincoln's call just arrived at the Northern Central's station. They'll have to march past here on their way to take the B&O rail line to Washington."

Alexander said, "I'm surprised they aren't sneaking through town in the middle of the night," and Harold laughed. Joseph wondered if they would ever stop snickering about how Abe Lincoln had come through Baltimore in the wee hours of the morning two months ago because of secessionist threats that he wouldn't reach Washington alive. And he might not have, judging from the mood of the people here today.

The noisy crowd was growing restless by the time someone shouted, "Here they come!"

Above the crescendo of hoots and hisses, a man yelled, "Down with Lincoln and his hirelings!" And then the air was full of echoing shouts and waving Confederate flags. A small U.S. flag was raised high, but two men tore it from its staff while others in the crowd began to pummel its owner.

"Serves him right," Harold said as the man made his escape, pushing his way past them while other spectators—including Alex—hooted and added their blows.

"He asked for it," Joseph agreed. Didn't everybody know that lately the surest way to start a fight was to raise a flag in the streets of Baltimore? Whether it was the Union's Stars and Stripes or the Confederacy's Stars and

Bars, someone was bound to take offense.

Now the crowd's attention was on the street again. The mass of people surged forward, then stopped so suddenly that Joseph stumbled into the man in front of him. A murmur went through the crowd like wildfire—*Police!*—and Joseph felt a rush of relief. He should have known the mayor would see to it that there wasn't any trouble. Maybe there wouldn't have been any danger to Abraham Lincoln, either.

"Hey, up there!" Alexander called to a group of men watching from an office window. "Can you see anything yet?"

One of them shouted back, "Just a column of troops with a line of policemen marching along on each side."

Raised fists in the crowd ahead of him and the increasing volume of the shouts and hisses told Joseph that the northern troops were passing, but to his disappointment, he couldn't see a thing.

"Next time, I'm going to be where I can see what's happening," Harold declared when the crowd began to break up. He glanced at the clock on the corner and added, "It's too late to go to the sweet shop—I'll see you fellows tomorrow."

Joseph was relieved. "See you tomorrow," he echoed, starting back down the street at a trot to get ahead of the disgruntled crowd. He'd have to hurry to get to the butcher shop before it closed.

On his way past the newspaper office, he paused long enough to read the bulletin that had been posted outside:

5

FORT SUMTER GARRISON
ARRIVES IN NEW YORK HARBOR;
MEN GIVEN HEROES' WELCOME

Pa would be interested in that news. He'd gone all the way to South Carolina last fall to help complete the brick-work and stonework inside Fort Sumter. For almost three months, he had lived in the unfinished barracks there with other masons from Baltimore, but he'd left soon after the Union soldiers moved in.

That was Pa, all right—giving up good money because he thought it was wrong to be paid for building some-thing he figured would be destroyed almost before the mortar set properly. Ma had hardly spoken to him for days after he'd arrived home. But when the news came that the soldiers who were defending Sumter—and the laborers who had stayed—were running short of food and fuel, Ma had to admit Pa had been smart to leave. Of course, it didn't hurt that by then he'd found work on the docks, loading and unloading merchant ships.

At the next corner, Joseph heard a boy call out, "Buy your evening paper and read all about it! Leaders here say 'Sumter business' is no cause for war."

Too bad it wasn't up to "leaders here" to decide that, Joseph thought as he hurried on. He didn't see much differ-ence between putting down a rebellion and fighting a war.

Pa had sent him to buy a paper when the news of the fort's bombardment came out earlier in the week, and he'd listened to every word. Ma had, too. And the most surprising thing had happened—she'd reached out to take Pa's hand!

"You're late today," the butcher said when Joseph arrived at the market. "Lucky for you I saved back some sausages. How is your mother's sprained ankle?"

"She says it's still badly swollen, and the skin's all purple."

The butcher shook his head. "That must make her life a lot more difficult."

And mine, too, Joseph thought. Since her fall down the stairs several days before, Ma was even more demanding than usual. He took the paper-wrapped package and handed over the coins. Most of the neighbors bought on credit, but Pa refused to. Said he'd go hungry before he'd owe money. Ma said he'd not be hungry very long before he changed his mind about that, but Joseph wasn't so sure. Pa was stubborn, and staying out of debt was important to him.

The sun was casting long shadows by the time Joseph ran up the front steps of the small row house near the harbor. What would his well-off classmates think if they saw where he lived? The downstairs was all one room, with the table where the family ate placed in front of the windows facing the street. Ma's worktable and the coal stove that served for heating and cooking were along the side wall with her rocking chair and Pa's easy chair nearby, and their bed and a chest were against the back wall. The upstairs was divided into two bedrooms, a small one in back that he shared with his older brother, Franz, and one in front for their three sisters. It was hard to imagine that some of the mansions where Franz delivered blocks of ice had twenty rooms or more—and all of them huge.

"So, Yosef," his mother said, giving his name its German pronunciation. "At last you decide to come home."

"Yes, ma'am." Why did his family insist on calling him *Yosef*? And why did his parents' sentences come out just different enough to mark them as foreign-born even though they had both been in America long enough to lose all but a trace of their accents?

From her rocking chair, Ma began the series of instructions he had come to expect. "Put the sausage by my dishpan and change out of your school clothes before you go for the water. After you have done that, Frieda and Erika need help with their lessons." The little girls looked up from their books, faces showing their envy that he didn't have to come straight home from school.

Joseph nodded, hoping his mother's ankle would be better soon so she wouldn't be so grumpy—and so she could do her own shopping. He was pretty sure his classmates' mothers had slaves—or maybe Irish servants—to do their shopping, and their chores, too. But Ma didn't need servants as long as she had him.

Franz no longer had to help around the house because he turned his wages over to Ma—most of his wages, anyway—and fifteen-year-old Anneliese turned over every penny she earned at the textile factory, so Ma never asked her to help, either. But Anneliese helped anyway, and

Joseph had decided that must be because she was a girl. He knew he'd be just like Franz and Pa and would never lift a finger around the house if he had worked all day.

As he climbed the narrow stairs to his room, Joseph thought resentfully of the way Ma never missed an opportunity to remind him that he could be working and bringing home money for the family if he didn't "go to that school with the rich men's sons." She was satisfied once her children could read and write English and had mastered enough arithmetic to keep the shopkeepers from cheating them. But Pa knew there was more to education. Pa wanted him to stay in school so he could work in an office or maybe even a bank instead of laying brick and stone in warm weather and working on the docks the rest of the year.

After Joseph put on a pair of neatly mended trousers and a shirt his brother had outgrown, he hung up his white shirt and brushed the jacket and trousers of his suit. In his school clothes, he looked as fine as any boy at the academy. Better than most, since he was tall and lean— not pudgy like Alexander. And Ma was so skilled with the scissors that no one would ever guess his wavy brown hair wasn't cut by a barber.

Joseph clattered down the stairs, picked up the water buckets, and headed for the pump at the corner. He was filling the second bucket when he saw Anneliese on her way home from work. His sister had loved school, and Joseph suspected that she envied him his scholarship. Franz, though, had gladly gone to work at fourteen—

Joseph's age. He had hated being confined to the class-room and was proud that in just three years he'd moved up from unloading the ice ships that arrived from Maine to loading blocks of ice onto the delivery wagons to having his own delivery route.

Anneliese waved to Joseph, and he waited for her. "How was school today?" she asked when they met.

"Fine," he said. "How was work?"

"The same as always."

Joseph was glad they had only half a block to walk, because he couldn't think of anything else to say. He was ashamed of his silent complaints about the few chores expected of him when his sister worked ten hours a day, six days a week in the textile factory and slipped on an apron as soon as she came home.

Later, at supper, Pa said, "While we were laying new paving stones on Pratt Street, we saw a Confederate flag go up on Federal Hill, and right away we saw it come down again. From across the harbor, we could hear the shouts— 'Down with the southern Confederacy!' and 'Hurray for the Union and Abe Lincoln!' We all cheered, too."

"On Howard Street, people were yelling, 'Down with Lincoln and his hirelings,' Joseph reported.

Anneliese said, "That reminds me—I heard the most ter-rible thing on my way home from work."

"And what was that most terrible thing, daughter?" Pa asked.

Ignoring his teasing tone, she announced, "A mob of secessionists shot at northern soldiers marching to

Camden Station this afternoon."

Franz spoke up. "That wasn't shooting, Anneliese, just some fools throwing firecrackers. I know, 'cause I was there."

Ma looked shocked. "You were in a secessionist mob when you should be working?"

With exaggerated patience, Franz said, "It was more of a crowd than a mob, and I wasn't *in* it, I was *watching* it. The street was blocked solid, and I couldn't drive my ice wagon through it."

"It was a crowd with firecrackers this time, but I think before many days pass, we will have mobs with guns," Pa said. "Today our foreman told us the newspaper says folks in the North want Lincoln to take over Maryland to make sure the secessionists—he calls them 'the secesh'—don't vote to join the Confederacy. I think they will make trouble, these secesh."

If they're all like Harold and Alex, they will, Joseph thought.

Franz said, "It wasn't just secesh in the crowd today. I caught sight of a couple Unionists from work. Some of the fellows are worried that northern troops answering the president's call to arms might decide to take things into their own hands when they get to Baltimore."

Pa sighed deeply. "One way or another, we will see trouble before this is over."

"We will if the newspapers keep printing things that make people in the North and the South hate each other," Ma said, passing Joseph the platter of bread.

Franz said, "Well, the news about Fort Sumter has certainly stirred things up. Everyone in the neighborhood is saying the government can't let those rebels get away with what they did. Lincoln's got to show 'em they can't fire on the American flag like that."

"The president's call for volunteers—seventy-five thousand of them, no?—ought to be a fair warning to the rebels," Pa said, spooning sugar into his coffee.

"I think this 'warning' is what led to the trouble here in Baltimore," Ma said. "And it will lead to trouble in this house if you or Franz think that you must go to Washington and volunteer. To join the militia or the City Guard and defend your home and family is one thing, but what happens in the South has nothing to do with us."

Joseph thought of what his history teacher had said about the rising threat of a civil war with Maryland as its battleground, but he decided not to mention that. He was glad when his brother spoke up. "Well, all those people yelling and throwing rocks at the northern troops this afternoon seemed to disagree with you, Ma."

She frowned and said, "Tomorrow, Yosef must stay away from the drunken secesh mobs uptown. It will not hurt for him to miss a day of school."

To Joseph's amazement, his father agreed. "It will be best for him to stay in the neighborhood for a day or two."

Joseph knew it would do no good to object, but he might be able to keep his mother from lining up a day of chores for him. "Then I'll have to study the next chapters in all my textbooks so I don't fall behind," he said.

In the silence that followed his words, Joseph glanced around the table. His mother's expression told him that she saw through his clumsy attempt to avoid helping around the house, and his little sisters' faces mirrored their envy. Both Anneliese and Franz seemed to be avoiding his gaze, but he was sure that they—and maybe even Pa, who was buttering a slice of bread—envied his unexpected day of freedom.

It was bad enough not to fit in at school, but it was worse not to fit into his own family.

CHAPTER TWO

"**I**'LL DO MY studying upstairs," Joseph said when breakfast was over the next morning.

"And ruin your eyes? When Frieda has cleared the table, you will study here, where the light is better," his mother said.

Joseph's spirits sagged. He knew he would feel her disapproval all day even if she never said a word. "I'll get you some more water while I'm waiting," he said, grabbing an empty bucket and making his escape. He hoped the city would be calm today so Pa would let him go back to school on Monday.

Joseph had been studying for almost two hours when Ma exclaimed, "Look what was under your chair!" She held up a spool of blue thread. "I think it fell from Mrs. Brunozzi's sewing basket when she came to visit yesterday."

"I'll take it to her if you want. It won't take long, and I can use a breather." He closed his book and slipped the spool into his pocket, pretending not to hear Ma mutter something about young people who need a breather from doing nothing.

Outside, the spring sunshine warmed the air, and at the corner he glanced across the harbor toward Federal Hill. The budding trees, pale green above the brighter carpet of grass, lifted his spirits. It was peaceful and uncrowded, the way he imagined the countryside must look. What must it be like to live in a house that stood by itself with grass all around it instead of one in the middle of a block-long row with the sidewalk at the foot of your front steps?

Hands in his pockets, Joseph set off toward Mrs. Brunozzi's boardinghouse. He was halfway there when a familiar voice called his name. What was Harold doing *here*? "How come you're not at the academy?" Joseph demanded, noticing the other boy was wearing his school clothes.

"Same reason you aren't, probably—I saw the news bulletin about another trainload of northern troops on the way through Maryland. A whole regiment from Massachusetts is coming in at President Street Station," Harold said, his voice excited.

"What time is the train due?" Joseph asked, realizing Harold didn't know this was the neighborhood he lived in, that Harold assumed he was playing hooky to see the northern troops arrive.

Harold shrugged. "Not for a while yet, but this time I want to be able to see what's happening. We won't be at the back of the crowd again today, right?"

"Right," Joseph echoed. Not that there were any signs of a crowd yet, and besides, the working-class people who lived around here weren't secessionists. Many of them were immigrants or the children of immigrants, proud to be Americans and grateful for the freedom and opportunity they had found here.

Walking at a good pace, the boys soon reached the station. "Listen—I hear a train coming," Harold said. "You think it's the troops?"

Joseph shrugged. "It could be, but it might just be a regular passenger train." Except that no scheduled trains arrived at this time on Friday mornings. When you lived within hearing distance of the station, you knew things like that. "Come on, let's go back to the train yard and see," he said, relieved that Harold hadn't seemed to notice his worn trousers and faded shirt.

By the time they dodged the wagon traffic on the busy street and made their way around to the tracks, the train's engine had been disconnected. A four-horse team was already hitched to the first of the cars, ready to pull it along the track of the street railway to the B&O station a mile to the west. The driver cracked his whip, and as the team set off at a trot, four more horses were hurried into place to be harnessed to the second car.

"It *is* the troops!" Harold cried when the first rail car turned out of the train yard and they could see uniformed men peering from the windows. "It's *them!*" And he let loose with a string of curses that would have earned Joseph a beating from Pa.

If all the secesh felt the way Harold did, it was a good thing the troops didn't have to walk to the B&O station, Joseph thought. And a good thing they had arrived earlier than expected. Even so, three young toughs stood near where the track turned into the street, jeering and shaking their fists. One of them shouted, "Hurray for Jefferson Davis, President of the Confederacy!" To Joseph's dismay, Harold yelled back, "Down with the United States and Abe Lincoln!"

"Look what they're doing," Joseph cried, pointing at the toughs running toward the car as if they intended to jump onto the front platform where the driver stood. They fell back when the driver lashed his whip at them, but they ran along next to the car, taunting the troops inside.

"Come on," Harold said. "Let's run with this next one."

What harm could that do? Joseph had often raced along the sidewalk on Monument Street just for the fun of it, trying to reach the corner before a car of the city's street railway did. He followed Harold, making sure to stay beyond the reach of the driver's whip. Farther up the street, the toughs had stopped to talk to a man on horseback. Joseph couldn't see the man's face but knew he was a stranger. No one who lived—or worked—near the harbor or the rail yard owned a horse.

"Hey, that's my cousin!" Harold exclaimed. "I thought he was going to the secession rally at Monument Square this morning." He waved his arms and shouted, "Hey, Randall! *Ran*dall!"

But Randall gave no sign that he'd heard. "He's headed back the way he came, riding lickety-split," Joseph said.

"On his way to spread the word that the troops came early, I'll bet," Harold said with satisfaction. "Sort of a modern-day Paul Revere, right? But instead of the British, this time it's the Yankees. Come on—let's run with the next car."

Harold began to fall behind after only half a block, but Joseph kept up with the railroad car a little longer. When it began to draw ahead of him, he stopped and raised his eyes to the windows. Some of the faces peering out looked frightened, some curious, and some angry. One soldier shook a fist at him.

Joseph was looking ahead to a group of men waiting at the corner when Harold came puffing up. "Let's rest a minute. We can have a go at the next car when it passes us."

"Right," Joseph agreed. It was good to be outside on a day like this—and on his own territory, he felt more at ease with Harold. Joseph looked back and saw a rail car approaching. Far behind it, another one had just pulled out of the train yard. How many were there? And how long would it take for them all to make the trip to the B&O station?

"Hey, look up there," Harold said. "I guess Cousin Randall spread the word, all right."

A crowd was gathering along Pratt Street, just beyond the wooden bridge. Joseph could hear the men's shouts, and he felt apprehensive. Where were the police this morning? He moved away from the track, positioning himself on the opposite side of the approaching rail car so Harold wouldn't ask why he didn't hiss and shout insults.

Thoroughly enjoying himself, Joseph ran along beside

car after car, keeping up as long as he could, and then dropping back to wait for the next one. By now, both sides of Pratt Street were lined with hissing, jeering men who made threatening gestures when the carloads of soldiers passed. Joseph could hardly believe the number of people swarming down the side streets to join the crowd. And it looked as if there was some kind of commotion opposite the wharf just beyond the next intersection, where a rail car had stopped.

"What's happening?" Harold asked when he caught up.

"I don't know, but that sounded like breaking glass."

"I'll bet somebody threw a rock at that last carful of Yankees!"

"Or maybe a paving stone," Joseph said, beginning to feel uneasy. This was the part of Pratt Street that was being repaired. "Look!" He pointed to a well-dressed man who had raised one of the heavy paving stones above his head and was about to hurl it. *What must Pa and the other masons repaving the street think of this? And where are they now?* Again Joseph heard the sound of splintering glass and a roar of approval from the growing crowd. A third stone crashed through a window of the rail car, and then two more landed harmlessly behind it as it finally pulled away.

Most of the crowd surged into the street and ran after the horse-drawn car, but a few men began to pry up more paving stones and heave them onto the track. Harold pointed toward a bustle of activity on the left and said, "Let's go see what those fellows are up to."

Harold took off at a trot, and glad to be away from the unruly crowd, Joseph followed him. "They're dragging something along the wharf," he said. "It looks like an anchor."

A man with a wheelbarrow full of sand called, "Hey, you two—stop gawking and make yourselves useful!"

"Sure," Harold said enthusiastically. "What should we do?"

"You can help them muscle that anchor at the end of the wharf the rest of the way over here," the man said, gesturing toward a cluster of people on the dock. "And your friend can take this load of sand and empty it on the rails."

Reluctantly, Joseph lifted the handles of the heavy wheelbarrow. *Now* what was he going to do? The wobble of the wheel gave him an idea, and he headed toward the track. But when he was still three or four yards away, he raised the wheelbarrow's left handle enough to unbalance the load and spill the sand some distance short of the rails.

His refusal to sabotage the track made no difference, though—except to him—because men had already piled paving stones on the rails and tossed lumber from the docks helter-skelter across them. The quick clopping of hooves and the hum of metal wheels on the rails told Joseph another car was approaching, and he caught his breath. What would happen when the rail car had to stop at the barricade? *Why didn't I think to run back to warn the driver?* He turned and saw that the man had stopped his team to unhitch the horses and was hurrying them to the rear of the car. Good. He was heading back to the station.

But now another car pulled up and blocked his way! While the second driver reversed his team, the men and boys who had lined up along the anchor rope managed to drag their load over from the dock and add it to the debris already on the track. When they saw that the cars had turned back, a few of the men shook their fists and shouted insults, and the rest thumped each other's backs and cheered. Joseph cheered, too, but he was cheering because the soldiers had escaped the wrath of the crowd. For the moment, at least.

"Tough luck," Harold said, eyeing the load of sand Joseph had spilled. "Now you can't say you helped show Abe Lincoln what happens when he tries to send his soldiers across Maryland."

"You can't very well say you helped, either," Joseph retorted. "Those cars had started back before you got that anchor halfway here." He saw Harold's scowl and quickly asked, "What do you want to do now? We'll never catch up to that last car that made it through, and the others have headed back to President Street Station."

His expression brightening, Harold said, "Let's go back there and see what happens next."

The boys sprinted to get in front of the crowd and then walked fast. With the track blocked, the rest of the troops would have to march to Camden Station to catch the Washington-bound train, but Joseph told himself it would be all right. After all, it was one thing to throw stones at a rail car and another to throw them at men armed with muskets.

Joseph walked faster, eager for a better look at the troops who had been so quick to answer the president's call for volunteers to put down the southern states' rebellion.

"Here they come!" Harold's voice was excited, and his usually pale skin was so flushed he looked feverish.

The Massachusetts volunteers marched toward them in columns of four, musket barrels resting on their shoulders, brass buttons and shoulder plates gleaming. Eyes straight ahead, they studiously ignored the howling crowd that surged around them. Where had so many people come from? And why weren't any policemen here to keep the peace? Joseph's jaw tightened when a man carrying a South Carolina flag forced his way to the front of the troops.

"That's rare!" hooted Harold. "He's making Lincoln's troops march behind a palmetto tree flag."

Joseph felt a surge of anger at the secessionist's audacity, and he almost cheered when a Unionist in the crowd pushed his way forward, grabbed the offending flag, and tore it from the pole. But he didn't keep his prize long. The crowd closed in around him, and after a brief scuffle, the torn flag was tied to the pole and held high again, though it was no longer in front of the marching troops. Joseph craned his neck, trying to see what had become of the man who had snatched it, and felt reassured when police raced from the station to rescue him from the angry crowd.

The first of the troops began to pass the boys, and Joseph felt a swell of pride and patriotism he didn't dare show. But by the time the last of the soldiers marched by him, his pride had changed to concern. Separated from the rest of their regiment, the northern men were greatly outnumbered by the howling crowd.

"Come on, let's follow them to Camden Station," Harold said, and he began to strut along behind the troops, much to the amusement of the men nearby.

"I'm going to try to get ahead of them," Joseph said, unwilling to watch Harold's parody of the northern soldiers.

"Good idea. By now, there will be even more people along the route. And this time, there aren't any policemen between us and the Yankees."

They set off at a trot to get ahead of the marching troops. They hadn't gone far when Harold said, "Hey, look up ahead. On the bridge."

Men with crowbars and axes were tearing up the planks and carrying them away! Joseph broke into a run. He stopped just before the bridge and saw that it was still passable, though the water below it was visible in places. On the far side of the span, a rowdy group of men and boys waited, shaking their fists and shouting threats at the rapidly approaching troops. The tramp of feet behind Joseph grew louder, and he moved aside. With a rush of fear, he wondered if the damaged structure would hold the weight of the marching column.

The men started across without hesitation, but their

ranks grew ragged as they were forced to step across the gaps left by the missing planks.

"Just look at 'em," Harold crowed. "They're doing the scotch hop!"

"We'll be doing it, too, if we follow 'em," Joseph reminded him. Jeers and catcalls from the crowd on the other side of the bridge filled the air, and Joseph realized how large the crowd had grown. He thought of his parents' warning the night before, then told himself that they wanted him to avoid the "drunken secesh mob uptown." Well, the route to Camden Station didn't go uptown—it was near the harbor the whole way.

The boys followed the last ranks of soldiers onto the bridge, and Joseph found himself stepping across the gaps where planks were missing, trying not to look at the water swirling below. He saw a group of neighborhood men that included the butcher's oldest son and one of the boarders from Mrs. Brunozzi's. They were shouting, "Go on back where you came from! Stay out of Maryland!"

So the crowd wasn't just the secesh, Joseph realized, and he hollered, "You'll be sorry you ever set foot in Baltimore!"

"It's about time you got in the spirit of things," Harold said. Raising his fist in the air, he yelled, "Death to Lincoln's hirelings!"

Joseph felt a chill. He was relieved when Harold's face lost its fierce expression and he said, "Let's drop back a little. I think I saw my uncle William up there, and I don't want him telling my father I wasn't at school today."

Joseph quickly agreed. He didn't like the looks of the jostling, shouting crowd that almost filled the street ahead of them, barely leaving room for the troops to pass. A boy his age aimed a slingshot and let a rock fly toward the marchers, and someone on the sidewalk threw a bottle that hit a bystander on the shoulder. Farther down the street, a woman flung a water pitcher from a balcony.

"Let's see if we can find something to throw, too," Harold said, his voice excited.

Joseph pretended to search along the curb, glad for an excuse to lag behind. Something sailed over his head, and he looked up to see a man hurling lumps of stove coal from an upstairs window.

At a shouted command, the troops began to march double time, and Harold looked back at Joseph and yelled, "Look at 'em run! I'll bet those muskets of theirs aren't loaded!"

The crowd went wild, and now the air seemed filled with missiles of all kinds—even a wooden stool thrown from a doorway. Joseph thought he heard shots, but he told himself it must be his imagination. He hurried after the troops, and his pulse raced when he saw that the entire road was barricaded not far ahead. *What will happen when the soldiers have to stop?*

A shot rang out in the crowd to Joseph's right, and then he heard a shouted order, followed by musket fire. His mouth went dry when he saw a man in a dark suit clutch his chest and drop a pistol as he crumpled to the ground. *I've just seen a man die.*

Beside him, Harold cried, "Did you see that? They shot him! Those Yankees just up and shot that man!"

"He fired at them first," Joseph protested, but Harold had already pushed his way to the edge of the crowd gathered around the dead man.

Now the northern troops were hurrying along Pratt Street, their muskets held in front of them, bayonets gleaming. The crowd scrambled back to let them by, then closed in behind them, its clamor louder and more abusive. Suddenly, Joseph was afraid. This wasn't a lark anymore—the crowd of protesters had become a mob, and he wanted no part of it.

But there was no turning back. The mass of men behind him carried Joseph along until he managed to stumble into the entry to a shop. He stood there, breathing hard, and watching the crowd surge past—was there no end to it? Two men struggled toward him through the jostling spectators on the sidewalk, half carrying a boy whose face was covered with blood.

"You there," one of the men called. "Hold that shop door open for us."

But shaken by the sight of the boy's limp body and blood-drenched shirt front, Joseph plunged back into the throng. One thought filled his mind: *That could have been Harold—or me.* He grabbed hold of a lamppost and clung to it, eyes closed, while he waited for a wave of nausea to pass. Men shoved their way by, cursing him for being in their way. Then, above the din, he heard someone call out, "It's the mayor!" Almost at once, other voices took up the shout, "Here comes the mayor!"

Mayor Brown will take charge, and then everything will be all right. Joseph opened his eyes and took a couple of deep breaths. No longer feeling ill, he shinnied up the lamppost in time to see the mayor—a known secessionist—shake hands with the officer leading the northern troops and then turn to march toward the B&O station beside him.

The worst of the shouting died down, and from his vantage point, Joseph saw the crowd fall back respectfully. Sensing this change of mood, he felt ashamed of his earlier panic. Someone called his name, and he saw Harold standing in the doorway of a store, gesturing for him to hurry. Joseph dropped to the sidewalk and pushed his way through the crush of sweating bodies toward his classmate.

Harold plunged ahead, weaving in and out of the crowd, and Joseph followed him. When he caught up, Harold asked, "Did you see Mayor Brown shake that Yankee's hand? I can't believe he's protecting the very troops we'll be fighting after Maryland secedes!"

"*If* Maryland secedes," Joseph reminded him as they pressed their way closer to the marching troops. "We'd do a lot better to stay neutral," he added, wondering if that would be possible after today. "Besides, it's the mayor's job to keep the peace in Baltimore, and it's his duty to protect the troops."

Harold frowned and said, "I guess you're right, but I'm not sure he can do it. Look—people have started throwing stones again."

It was true—the crowd was getting bolder. Joseph

gasped when he saw a rioter grab a soldier's musket, wrench it away, and fire it at him. The soldier slumped to the ground, and Joseph cried out, "That's *murder*!" He could hardly make his mouth form the words.

"Soldiers have to be prepared to die, you know," Harold said, his voice shaky.

"In a battle, yes. But not like that." *He was just marching along, and somebody killed him!*

"Come on—something's happening up ahead," Harold said.

Joseph kept up with Harold as they hurried along the fringes of the crowd, dodging a couple of ragged children. It wasn't long before a word came rippling back to them: *Police.*

"My cousin Randall says practically everybody on the police force is secessionist, from the marshal on down," Harold said, his voice excited. "What do you think they'll do?"

"Their job, I hope," Joseph answered as the marshal and more policemen than Joseph had ever seen at one time came running from the direction of Camden Station, revolvers drawn. When they massed between the troops and the mob that tormented them, their tall hats made them look huge, and their expressions made it clear they wouldn't hesitate to use their weapons.

"Keep back!" the marshal shouted. "Keep back, or we'll shoot!"

A rioter tried to run past the solid line of police officers, but the marshal seized him. The crowd began to draw back, and Harold said, "Looks like the fun is over for today." But no sooner had he said it than shots were fired from somewhere in front of the troops. His eyes brightened, and he said, "Let's run up there and see what's happening."

More shots were fired, and Joseph hung back. Pa always said it was foolish to go looking for trouble. "I have a better idea—let's take a short cut to the station. Come on." Without giving Harold a chance to disagree, Joseph led the way down Hanover to Camden Street. As soon as they rounded the corner, they could see a mass of people milling around the station two blocks ahead.

"How did they get here before we did?" Harold asked, slowing to a walk.

"Those must be the people who followed the rail cars when we went back to President Street Station," Joseph said. That seemed a long time ago, but it couldn't have been more than an hour before.

By the time they were opposite Camden Station, the boys could see another contingent of policemen trying to protect the cars of the Washington-bound train and keep the mob from blocking the track ahead of it. "Let's run a ways down the track and drag some branches or something onto it," Harold said.

"I've had enough running for one day," Joseph told him. "I'll just wait here for the marchers."

"Then I guess I will, too," Harold agreed. "Look—here they come."

The boys watched the troops force their way through the crowd that had arrived earlier and head for the cars that would take them to the capital city. Behind the soldiers, the police marshal and his men tried to hold back the mob that spilled into Howard Street and surged toward the station. Stones still flew, and Joseph said, "I wouldn't want to be one of those policemen."

"Neither would I," Harold agreed. "Can you imagine having to protect your enemies? Look—there's Alexander." He raised his voice and called, "Hey, Alex!"

Joseph's heart sank when the other boy began making his way toward them.

"Those Yankees shot one of my neighbors," Alexander said as he crossed the street.

"Just shot him for no reason at all?" Joseph asked.

Alexander glared at him and said, "He'd grabbed their flag, but I don't think that's reason enough to shoot somebody, do you?"

"Is he dead?" Harold asked before Joseph could answer.

"He was hit in the leg," Alexander said. "Last I saw, a couple of men from his office were carrying him off."

They hadn't shot to kill, then. "Sounds like the train's about to leave," Joseph said when he heard the hiss of the engine building up steam.

"Let's give 'em the send-off they deserve," Alexander urged. "You coming with us, Joe?"

Joseph shook his head. "Let 'em leave. I have no quarrel with northern men—provided they don't try to take over Maryland."

"Always playing neutral, aren't you?" Alexander said, his voice hostile.

"Aw, leave him alone, Alex," Harold said. "As long as he's not a Unionist, he's okay, right?"

Alexander gave Joseph a challenging glance and echoed, "As long as he's not a Unionist."

Except he *was* a Unionist. Joseph watched his two class-mates dash across the street and shoulder their way through the mass of people toward the station platform. He waited until the locomotive's huge wheels began to turn before he started home, wondering why he felt like such a humbug for going along with Harold. Other Unionists were in the crowd, after all.

"But I never let on that I don't feel the same way Harold does about Lincoln's volunteers," Joseph muttered. The words *As long as he's not a Unionist, he's okay* seemed to ring in his ears, and he thought, I'll be a complete outcast at school if the other boys find out the truth. Maybe Ma's right that people should "stay with their own kind." The trouble is, I don't have anything in common with my old pals in the neighborhood now that they have jobs or apprenticeships. Besides, when I'm free on Saturdays, they have to work, and when they're free in the evenings, I have to study.

Deep in thought, Joseph almost bumped into one of the Pratt Street merchants standing on the sidewalk outside his shop, watching a few stragglers on their way toward the station and remnants of the crowd making their way back uptown. The merchant brushed aside his apologies and asked, "Do you know if the troops got off all right?"

"I saw the train leaving the station. The police managed

to hold back the crowd so the rest of the men could board the cars, but some boys I know were planning to run along the tracks for a ways."

The shopkeeper swore under his breath and then said, "What's wrong with all those southern sympathizers? Can't they see that this city's future lies with the North? Where do they think I buy the goods I sell? And who do they think buys most of what we produce in our factories? If this state secedes, we'll all regret it, mark my words."

"I'll regret it, all right," Joseph agreed. "I think Maryland should side with the Union." How good it felt to say that!

The driver of a passing delivery wagon called out, "Did you hear the news? Virginia troops have taken over the arsenal at Harper's Ferry!"

The shopkeeper swore more loudly this time. "That's where the U.S. government stored its weapons, you know," he told Joseph. "Lincoln might have been able to write off the bombardment of Sumter as the work of South Carolina's fire-eaters, but he won't be able to ignore this. Imagine *Virginians* throwing their lot with the Confederacy!"

Farther down the block, the wagon driver was calling out the news of Harper's Ferry to a small knot of men who had gathered at the corner. "I'd better go," Joseph said, hoping they weren't planning to make more trouble. Slowing as he passed them, he caught the words *over a hundred killed.*

One of the younger men saw him and said, "Hey, here's the boy who spilled that barrow load of sand. Have you heard about the casualties? Those Yankees killed more than a hundred men!"

"At Harper's Ferry?" Joseph asked.

"Here in Baltimore!" the man said, looking at him as though he were crazy. "The next trainload of Lincoln's hirelings will pay for this."

Shaken, Joseph went on his way. A hundred Baltimore citizens dead! Was that possible? Wouldn't he have heard more gunfire—or seen more bodies? At the sound of hoofbeats, he looked up to see Harold's cousin galloping toward him, shouting out to everyone he passed. Still playing Paul Revere, Joseph thought as Randall clattered past, calling, "Troops from New York arriving any minute at President Street Station!"

The next trainload of Lincoln's hirelings will pay for this.

Joseph was staring after Randall when the man who had spoken those words ran past with his friends. "Come on, young fellow," he called over his shoulder. "Didn't you hear about the troops?"

Joseph had heard, but this time he wasn't going to get involved. He'd had enough violence for one day. Maybe even forever. It seemed a long time since he'd left home on a quick errand for Ma. He checked to make sure the spool of thread was still in his pocket, and when he felt it, he headed for Mrs. Brunozzi's boardinghouse.

CHAPTER THREE

T WENTY MINUTES later, Joseph was on the way home from Mrs. Brunozzi's when Franz shouted to him from his ice wagon. After he guided his horse to the curb, Franz said, "I thought you'd be at home, studying."

"And I thought you'd be delivering ice in the rich people's neighborhoods," Joseph said, climbing up to the seat beside his brother. "What are you doing in our part of town?"

"The militia's been called out to keep the peace," Franz said. The wagon began to roll again, and he added, "Soon as I take this rig back to the ice company, I'll stop by home for my uniform."

Joseph heard the note of excitement in his brother's voice. "If you want, I can rub down your horse and give her some oats to save you a little time, but it's a bit late to think about keeping the peace. Haven't you heard about the riot?"

"That's why the governor's called out the militia," Franz said. "They're saying the troops killed more than three hundred secesh. Hey, where's everybody going?"

Following his gaze, Joseph said, "To President Street Station, probably. A bunch of New York troops are due to arrive any minute."

"They must already be there. Listen to the shouting."

Joseph frowned. "I didn't hear a train come in, did you?"

"No, but we might as well swing by the station and have a look." Franz urged the horse past a freight wagon and turned toward President Street.

The bleat of police whistles and shouts of the crowd made Joseph's breath come faster. His brother stopped the ice wagon by the rail yard, and Joseph saw that in spite of the efforts of the police, the mob had smashed train windows and men were hurling rocks into the cars. Rioters jumped up and down on the tops of some cars, and a man was trying to beat his way in through the roof of one with a metal bar. Seeing the terrified faces at the windows, Joseph cried, "But those men aren't soldiers!"

A rioter cradling an armload of bricks called over his shoulder, "They ain't in uniform, but they're on their way to Washington to fight for 'Ape' Lincoln, just the same."

Joseph heard galloping hoofbeats and saw the police marshal and a stern-looking older man wearing a military uniform. When the two of them rode into the rail yard, the rioters grew quiet. A few slunk away, but most came closer to hear what the marshal had to say.

After he'd introduced his companion, a general with the Maryland state militia, the police marshal said, "The men in these train cars are unarmed volunteers from

Pennsylvania. They pose no threat to the citizens of Baltimore, but we're going to send them back where they came from anyway. I want all of you to go home so the general and I can make arrangements to do that."

Pennsylvanians, then, and not New Yorkers, Joseph thought as the crowd began to thin. You couldn't believe half of what you heard. He took a deep breath and said, "Boy, I'm glad that's over."

"I'm not so sure it is," his brother said as they headed toward the ice company. "A lot of the rioters are still hanging around. I'll take you up on your offer to look after Nelly so I can report for militia duty a bit sooner."

"Tell Ma I'll be home in a little while," Joseph said. He didn't want to think about what she would say when he got there. He'd already been gone a couple of hours on an errand that should have taken twenty minutes at the most.

After he had rubbed down the horse and given her oats and a bucket of water, Joseph left the ice company stable. He glanced across the harbor to Federal Hill and thought how peaceful it looked. What must it be like to live on one of the estates over there? Or even to work at the hilltop signal station with its view of approaching ships?

Joseph had almost reached the corner of the street where he lived when he heard the thud of running feet and looked back to see a group of laborers from the docks pounding toward him. He pressed himself against the wall of a building to give them room to pass, and then, curiosity getting the better of him, he followed them, sure he would end up at President Street Station—for the third time that day.

Just as he'd thought, that was where they were headed. The train yard was a scene of chaos, and Joseph stood a safe distance away to watch the frightened-looking Pennsylvanians being hurried from the passenger cars and loaded into windowless freight cars. Many of the men were bleeding, and a few were half carried by their companions. A woman standing in her doorway called to Joseph and said, "Some of the ones without uniforms have slipped away. I counted half a dozen."

"Don't much blame 'em," Joseph said, his eyes on the melee. Nearby, neighborhood men exchanged punches with well-dressed men from uptown, and a railroad worker grabbed the arm of a roughly dressed fellow who was about to throw a rock at the volunteers.

Joseph had been in his share of fistfights in the neighborhood, and in the school yard, too. But those were fair fights, and they were fought in anger, not hatred. At least not the kind of hatred he'd seen today. But in spite of the revulsion he felt, he couldn't bring himself to leave. There was something fascinating about seeing grown men completely out of control, something exciting about the violence—and about not knowing what might happen next—that drew him like a magnet.

At last the northbound train pulled out of the station, and the crowd roared its approval. Some of the cheering secessionists waved Confederate flags, and others continued to throw stones at the departing freight cars. People on the fringes of the crowd began to drift away, and Joseph caught scattered phrases: . . . *Close to five hundred of our citizens killed . . . revenge . . . arm ourselves against . . .*

three o'clock at Monument Square . . .

The sound of the train faded away, but Joseph noticed that the din in the station yard had increased. Some of the rioters, angry at being deprived of their prey, attacked the remaining freight cars and began breaking out the windows in unoccupied passenger cars. Pa said vandalism was the coward's crime, and if you couldn't stop it, you shouldn't dignify it by watching.

Joseph turned away in disgust. Maybe he'd walk up to Monument Square and stake out a place where he could hear what the speakers had to say. Squinting, he glanced at the sky. Must be about two o'clock—no wonder he was so hungry. But this was the most exciting day he'd ever had—well worth missing a meal for.

On the way to Monument Square, he saw a crowd of men milling around outside a building and crossed the street to avoid them. When he read the sign over the building's door, he understood: It was the armory of one of the militia units. But were those militia members waiting for their officers to arrive, or were they rioters hoping to break in and take the weapons that were stored there? Joseph felt a chill at the thought of an armed mob raging through the city's streets.

People were already gathering in the square around the monument to George Washington when Joseph got there. More and more men arrived, and the buzz of conversation grew louder, but there was no shouting or name calling. This was an orderly crowd, though Joseph sensed an undercurrent of excitement.

At last the meeting began. Joseph listened while first the police marshal and then the mayor urged the people to stay calm. Finally, a man Joseph didn't recognize climbed to the base of the monument to speak, and a ripple of excitement flowed through the crowd: *The governor!*

Standing beneath the Maryland state flag, the governor, too, spoke of calm. The people packed into the square listened quietly at first, but when he announced that to avoid more bloodshed, he would see that northern soldiers were kept out of Baltimore, the cheers were almost deafening. Joseph cheered as loudly as anyone, and he joined in the roar of approval when the governor declared, "I am a Marylander, and I love my state, and I love the Union, but I will suffer my right arm to be torn from my body before I will raise it to strike a sister state."

How Joseph envied the governor's courage—he'd faced a mostly secesh crowd and told them that he loved the Union. *He* didn't even have the courage to say that in front of the boys at school. But then, *he* couldn't win their approval by promising to keep northern troops out of the city. Or by assuring them that any Maryland troops sent to Washington would be used to protect the city rather than against the southern states.

The crowd had begun to break up, and Joseph turned toward home, feeling a lot better about being a Unionist—and about telling the boys at school he wanted Maryland to be neutral. After all, that was what the governor wanted, and the people had cheered for him.

Joseph was almost home when he heard a commotion

behind him. He glanced back and saw a stranger who looked no older than Franz running along the sidewalk on the other side of the street with three older youths in close pursuit. When they passed opposite him, Joseph recognized the young toughs he'd seen at the train yard that morning. *That must be one of the Pennsylvania volunteers they're after!*

The four of them disappeared around the next corner, but Joseph knew the pursuers had caught up to their intended victim by their cries of triumph. At the cross street, he saw that the largest of the roughnecks was holding the stranger while the others pummeled him mercilessly. The struggling youth managed to land a kick on the shins of one of his tormenters, with the result that the two of them began aiming kicks as well as blows at him, while the third gave his arm a cruel twist.

Now the youth no longer tried to resist, but the toughs continued their merciless pounding. *If they keep that up, they'll kill him!* Joseph dashed diagonally across the street and charged head down into the fray, knocking one of the attackers into another. They fell like tenpins, but the third roughneck shoved the limp form of their victim aside and lunged for Joseph.

He ran for his life. *He'll grab me and the other two will catch up and they'll—* Shouts and the sound of running feet told him the toughs were gaining. The rasping breath of the one in the lead was so close Joseph could almost feel the viselike grip of fingers closing on his shoulder.

A lamppost stood just ahead of him, and with an extra

burst of speed, he cut to the right of it, reached out to grab the post with his left hand, and swung around to face the way he had come—and his pursuers. He thrust out a foot and tripped the one in the lead, who crashed to the sidewalk. The second tough leaped over Joseph's outstretched foot and almost stumbled, but the third made a grab for him.

He wrenched away and ran faster than he ever had before, but his pursuer was faster still. The next thing Joseph knew, he was in a stranglehold, and the more he kicked and struggled to free himself, the tighter his captor's grip became. As if in a dream, Joseph saw another figure in front of him, fist drawn back and eyes dark with rage. The grip around his neck was so tight he could scarcely breathe, and his pulse pounded in his ears. *I'm going to die.*

But at the shrill bleat of a whistle, the tough who was holding Joseph shoved him away and yelled, "Police!" All three bullies took off, and Joseph collapsed to the sidewalk, gasping in huge gulps of air.

"Are you all right?" called the young stranger, limping toward him.

Joseph struggled to his feet. "I—think so. What about yourself?"

"It's a good thing you came along when you did," the youth said. "I couldn't have taken any more of their punishment." Already one eye was nearly swollen shut, and he held a bloodstained handkerchief to his badly cut lip.

"If the police hadn't been nearby, those rowdies would

have beaten us both to a pulp," Joseph said. "We'd better get away from here. Come on, I live nearby."

"I'm much obliged," the young man said. "I've not been away from home before, and—"

Another bleat of a whistle, this one much closer, made them both jump. No officers were in sight, but a small boy was watching them from an open window of the house at the end of the row. "Pa got me a pennywhistle," the child said, holding it up. "See?"

Joseph's nervous laugh was cut short by the sound of shouts followed by what might have been a pistol shot. "Quick!" he said, glancing over his shoulder. "Around the corner." He would have raced for home if his companion hadn't been limping so badly. At least they didn't have far to go. "My name's Joseph Schwartz, by the way. I live in the middle of the block."

"Jonathan Engle, from Pennsylvania. My father's a farmer. I'd never been in a city till my militia unit answered Lincoln's call."

"And I've never been on a farm," Joseph said. "Here we are." He led the way up the few steps to the door and opened it. "Ma?" he called, "I'm home, and—"

"Such a long time it took you to return a spool of—"

"This is Jonathan Engle from Pennsylvania," Joseph said, interrupting. "The secesh were beating him up, so I brought him here."

Ma gasped when she saw the young man's ripped and bloody clothing and his bruised face. "The poor boy!" She turned to Joseph's sisters and said, "Frieda, bring warm water from the kettle, and you, Erika, find clean rags and a towel. Joseph, go and get your brother's extra work shirt for Jonathan to wear while his own is washed and mended."

On his way upstairs, Joseph thought, If I hadn't come along, Jonathan would be lying on the sidewalk back there, half dead. And if that little boy's father hadn't bought him a penny whistle— He shuddered.

Joseph took his brother's extra shirt from the peg on the wall and went downstairs, where he found his mother and Jonathan deep in conversation—in German.

"You see, Yosef," Ma said in English, "your Jonathan is not ashamed to speak the language of the old country. And it does not make him less of an American." She turned her attention back to Jonathan and said something that made him laugh, something Joseph didn't understand.

It was nearly dark by the time Ma had cleaned all of Jonathan's cuts, put poultices on the worst of his bruises, and instructed Frieda to wash his shirt in cold water and rub salt into any bloodstains that didn't scrub out. "Anneliese should be at home by now, and so should your father," she said, frowning at Joseph as though he were responsible for their absence.

Anneliese shouldn't be out on the streets alone. "I'll go and meet—"

"You will go nowhere!" Ma said, and Joseph was steeling himself for a tongue-lashing when the door opened and his father and older sister came in.

After the introductions, Pa turned to Joseph and said, "I saw you near Camden Station today, Yosef."

So Pa had followed the rioters, too. "Yes, sir. I stayed away from uptown like you and Ma said."

Ma glared at him from the stove, where she was stirring a pot of stew. "You were supposed to stay away from *trouble.*"

Pa said, "I think Yosef did that, the same as I did. I watched from inside a barbershop, and he stayed across the street from where the trouble was. And when the other lads went to join the mob, I saw him turn away."

Pa wouldn't be so pleased with me if he knew I'd run with the mob—or if he'd seen me pushing that wheelbarrow load of sand.

"And then Joseph got me out of some real trouble," Jonathan said.

Ma began to ladle up the stew. "You see, Anneliese?" she said, glancing at her daughter. "That is how it is with the men. They stick up for each other, no matter what."

"I might be dead if Joseph hadn't stuck up for me," Jonathan said, and he proceeded to describe how Joseph had rescued him. When he finished, Ma's face was pale and Pa's was grave, but Joseph's sisters were looking at him with rapt admiration.

"And then a little kid rescued me," Joseph said, embarrassed by all the attention focused on him.

When he finished telling about the boy with the whistle, his father said solemnly, "This story could have had a different ending for our two young men here."

Pa called me a young man.

"And to think that we kept Yosef home from school

44

because we wanted him safe here in the neighborhood," Ma said. "I think there is no safe place in these troubled times." She smoothed her apron and said, "But come, all of you. The girls have put the food on the table."

Joseph passed the platter of bread and asked, "Were there still rioters in the streets when you left work, Anneliese?"

She shook her head. "Patrols of militiamen were everywhere, but I was still glad Pa came to walk me home. We saw Franz, by the way. He was standing at a corner with a musket on his shoulder, but he pretended not to notice us."

Pa chided her, saying, "Your brother was on duty, Anneliese. He must not seem to be distracted by a pretty girl, even if she is his sister." Then he turned to Jonathan and Joseph. "You had good luck that only three fellows were in the group that fought you. I hear that bands of older boys, some of them with weapons stolen from the gun shops, are on the streets. But now it seems that things are under control. For the time being, at least."

"And what is this 'for the time being'?" Ma asked. "Is the trouble over, or is it not?"

Pa hesitated a moment before he answered. "Some say northern troops are gathering in Philadelphia and Harrisburg, and that they will come to punish Baltimore for the way their state's unarmed militiamen were treated here. Boys like this Jonathan of ours."

Joseph saw a look of fear cross Anneliese's face. "That might be just a rumor," he said, thinking of how the number of citizens killed in the riot was larger each time he heard it. Erika tugged at his sleeve, and when he leaned toward her, she whispered a question in his ear. "Why don't you ask him yourself?" he whispered back.

Erika turned to the young Pennsylvanian and asked shyly, "If you're a soldier, how come you don't have on a uniform?"

"When we volunteered, they told us we'd be given everything we'd need when we got to Washington," Jonathan explained.

"If those volunteers from Massachusetts hadn't had their weapons, they wouldn't have gotten to Washington," Joseph said. "Not alive, anyway." Before anyone could respond to that, there was a brisk knock at the door, and he went to see who was there. To his surprise, he found himself facing a policeman.

"Some of the Pennsylvania recruits never made it onto the train taking them back home, so we're going house to house, trying to round up the stragglers. Are you harboring any?"

"What are you going to do with them?" Joseph asked, stalling. With their marshal leading them, the police had protected the northern volunteers from the rioters—but what if their Confederate sympathies got the better of them now, unsupervised in the dark streets?

The officer glared at Joseph and said, "We're sending them home, like the mayor said we would."

Joseph's father joined them at the door. "My son has rescued an injured Pennsylvania boy and brought him here to safety. We will walk with him to the station when he has finished his meal."

Joseph heard the note of pride in his father's voice when

he said *my son*, and he hoped Ma and the girls had heard it, too.

An hour later, Joseph and Pa were leaving President Street Station after waiting to see the train steam off for the north. The rubble-strewn train yard had seemed strangely sinister in the darkness, and Joseph was glad he wasn't there alone.

"Thanks to you, Jonathan is better off than many of those young men," Pa said as they headed home. "Some of them looked like they had seen battle."

Joseph thought of Ma's words when she handed Jonathan his washed and mended shirt after Anneliese had ironed it dry: *At least your poor mother will not have to see her boy all bloodied.* "It's hard to believe that something like this could happen," he said, thinking of all the violence he had witnessed that day, remembering the boy covered with blood, realizing that only by luck had he escaped a similar fate.

After a moment Pa said, "What I saw today does not surprise me much. The men who write in the newspapers, they had turned North and South against each other long before Union men moved into that fort in Charleston Harbor. And now—"

"Pa, look." A group of men was coming their way, light from the gas streetlamps throwing hulking shadows far in front of them. Joseph's heart began to pound. What if those toughs had come back and brought their friends? Would they recognize him in the dark? He breathed more easily when one of the shadowy figures called, "Is that you, Schwartz?"

"It is," Pa called back. "And who is asking?"

"Kelly, and some others from the neighborhood. We just stopped by your house."

When they met under a streetlamp, Joseph recognized several of their neighbors with a uniformed man he'd never seen before. The stranger introduced himself and said, "I'm looking for volunteers to come with my unit and stand by in case they're needed for a job that's crucial to the safety of this city."

Mr. Kelly said, "There's threats from the North to send troops to lay Baltimore in ashes—payment for what the secesh did here today."

Then what Pa told us wasn't a rumor.

Frowning at the interruption, the officer continued. "Your son Franz suggested that you and your neighbors might provide some of the manpower we'll need if we get orders to burn the railroad bridges to prevent those threats from being carried out. Will you come?"

"Of course." Pa put a hand on Joseph's shoulder and said, "Tell your mother I will be back when my help is no longer needed."

"Can't I come along, Pa?"

"Tonight your duty is to protect your mother and the girls."

At least he didn't say I was too young, Joseph thought as he watched the men head toward Pratt Street. He weighed the idea of following them at a distance, but the word *duty* hung heavy in the air, and he set off for home.

CHAPTER FOUR

JOSEPH STRUGGLED awake the next morning, stiff from sleeping in Pa's easy chair—fully dressed and with the stove poker close at hand. Yawning, he got up and reached for the water buckets. For once, Ma wouldn't have to nag him out of bed to fill them for her and carry in coal for the stove.

Only Mr. Kelly's youngest son was at the pump ahead of him, and while Joseph waited his turn, he glanced across the harbor. Federal Hill was close enough as the crow flies, but it was almost as far out of his reach as the moon. He'd feel no more at ease with the well-off folks who owned estates on Federal Hill than he did with the rich boys at school. *Yesterday, though, Harold seemed just like any other fellow.*

Home again, he dipped water from the bucket into the coffee pot. He was congratulating himself on his thoughtfulness when his mother said, "Next time you are up before me, start the fire before you go for the water. Then the stove can heat up while you're at the pump." She limped to her worktable and began to scoop flour into a bowl. "Do you think you can be back before dark if I ask you to walk Anneliese to work this morning?"

"I ought to be able to manage that," Joseph said, matching her sarcasm with his words but keeping his tone of voice respectful. He half expected a reprimand, but Ma only gave him a sharp look.

More than an hour later, on his way back from walking his sister to the textile factory, Joseph detoured past the newspaper office to see if any bulletins had been posted. Standing at the edge of the group that had gathered to wait for the latest news, he could see only the large print at the top:

TWELVE CITIZENS, FOUR SOLDIERS KILLED IN RIOTING; SCORES INJURED

I knew it couldn't be as many as people were saying. Joseph eased his way closer so he could read more:

BRIDGES BURNED ON ALL RAIL LINES LEADING NORTH

So they'd done it, Joseph thought, glad to know the city was safe from the rage of northerners who had heard about the Union men killed or injured in the riots. He pressed his way forward until he could read the rest of the bulletin:

CITY TO BUY WEAPONS
FOR ITS DEFENSE
Citizens Will Be Armed
To Repel Invaders

He was reading it all a second time when a voice at his elbow said, "What are you doing up so early on a Saturday?"

Harold. Joseph shrugged and said, "Same thing you are, I guess. Trying to find out what's going on. I already knew about the bridge burning," he added. "My father was in on it." Maybe next time Alexander accused him of being a Unionist, Harold would remember that.

"My father was meeting with the mayor and the governor half the night," Harold said. "When I got up, I found a note asking me to check for news bulletins first thing this morning. Listen, I've got to get back—Cook hates it when I'm late for breakfast."

"See you on Monday, then," Joseph said. He remembered that Harold's father had something to do with one of the railroads and wondered if Mr. Porter's meeting had been to decide whether the bridges should be burned. "Rich men make the decisions and poor men carry them out," he muttered as he set off for home.

He'd walked only a short distance before he met another boy from his class. "Going to check the bulletins, Charles?" he asked.

Charles nodded. "My mother asked me to. She's upset because of all the commotion in the city even though it's nowhere near where we live. Well, see you on Monday."

After they said good-bye, Joseph realized that this was the most he'd ever heard Charles say at one time. Unlike the other boys at school, he rarely joined in the arguments and discussions in the school yard. Once Alexander had made fun of him behind his back, but Harold had said, "Let it go, Alex," and it hadn't happened again.

When he passed President Street Station, Joseph saw a man sweeping up broken glass in the train yard and tossing debris into a wheelbarrow. Thinking that this might be a chance to earn a little pocket money, he found the stationmaster and said, "If you're hiring extra help to clean up after the trouble yesterday, I could work for you, sir."

"I could use someone to sort through the baggage cars to see what can be salvaged and whether we can identify the owners. You game for that?"

"Yes, sir," Joseph said, and he followed the stationmaster through the building and out to the train yard where the boxcars were lined up. "The secesh did all this?" He stared at the damaged cars and the debris that surrounded them.

The stationmaster said, "The damage was done by the secesh, but some of the looting was done by folks from the neighborhood." He picked up a flattened object that had once been a trumpet and said, "It's a shame what they did here—pretty much destroyed the instruments of the Sixth Massachusetts Regimental Band. Somebody must have jumped up and down on that drum over there."

Joseph's eyes strayed to an empty boxcar that had its

door pried open and he said, "Looks like they carted off whatever was inside that one."

"It was filled with boxes of muskets and ammunition," the stationmaster told him, "and it was the police who carried it all away. The officers claimed the weapons would be used for the city's defense, but if you ask me, they could as easily end up in rebel hands across the Virginia border." He sighed and said, "Well, young man, you have your day's work cut out for you. Start by sorting things into two piles—one for discards and one for anything that can be salvaged, all right?"

Joseph nodded and set to work, realizing that the stationmaster hadn't said what his pay would be. Well, it was sure to be more than enough to treat his classmates at the sweet shop next time he was invited. And just being out of the house so Ma couldn't order him around all day was worth something.

By midday, he had a large pile of discards and a much smaller one of undamaged goods. He looked up as the stationmaster paused beside him and said, "On your noon break, run up to the newspaper office and see if any bulletins have been posted, would you?"

"Yes, sir!" That would give him an excuse to leave the house again as soon as he finished eating.

Even before he reached home, Joseph could smell the yeasty aroma of freshly baked bread, and when he went inside, he saw steam rising from the stew pot on the stove.

"Set out another bowl, Erika," Ma said. "Your brother will honor us with his presence."

Erika gave him a reproachful look, but Joseph ignored her. "Didn't I tell you I could manage to be back before dark, Ma?" He took his place at the table and asked, "Franz and Pa aren't home yet?"

"Your brother is asleep after his night of patrolling the streets, but your father and the other volunteers from the neighborhood have not come back."

Frieda piped up and said, "Mrs. Kelly thinks they've all been captured by the men from Pennsylvania."

"She was crying," Erika added.

Ma rolled her eyes. "Mrs. Kelly cries just like *that*," she said, snapping her fingers. "Did you forget Franz told us the men did not go to burn those bridges until a few hours before dawn? Of course they are not back yet, Erika! And you need not worry about your pa—he can take care of himself."

"I wish he hadn't gone," Erika said, her voice trembling.

"You are a foolish girl," Ma said. "What kind of man refuses to do what is needed to protect his home and family? Do you *want* angry Pennsylvanians marching into Baltimore? Laying the city in ashes? That is the threat Franz said they made."

Erika began to sob, and Joseph wasn't sure whether it was Ma's scolding tone or her words, but when Frieda burst into tears, he decided it must be the image of Baltimore in flames. "With the railroad bridges destroyed, there's no way for the trains to bring the soldiers here," he said. Then he glanced at his mother and said, "Good stew, Ma."

"It is always better on the second day."

Joseph spooned up the last of it before he announced, "I'm going up to the newspaper office to see if they've posted any more bulletins. The stationmaster asked me to check," he added when he saw his mother's frown. "I'm working for him this afternoon."

Her forehead smoothed. "At last you take your nose from the books long enough to bring home a few coins," she said.

He would have to hand over his afternoon wages, Joseph realized, but he'd hold back what he'd earned this morning.

Just as he reached Pratt Street, a group of uniformed men on horseback rode past. Cavalry! He was still watching them when a barber standing outside his shop spoke to him. "They're from Frederick—I saw their company flag. I hear that a couple of units from Baltimore County have come into town, too."

"Add them to all the city's militia units, and we ought to be in good shape," Joseph said. He noticed that a Maryland state flag flew from the pole over the barber's door instead of the American flag that had been there ever since South Carolina seceded.

The barber nodded. "From what I hear, men all over town are volunteering. It's a madhouse outside the armories."

"Aren't you going to volunteer?" Joseph asked.

The man shook his head. "I'm a Unionist."

"My pa's a Unionist, and he volunteered."

The barber shrugged. "I have a business to run. With all the excitement, not many customers stopped by yesterday or this morning, but when things settle down a bit, I'm counting on the officers of these out-of-town units coming in for a shave."

Joseph crossed the street and continued on his way. He couldn't blame the barber for replacing his U.S. flag, since flying the Stars and Stripes would be a signal for rowdies to vandalize his shop. But it didn't seem right for a man to shirk his duty in the hope of making money from the city's troubles.

Most of the shops Joseph passed were closed, and some had their windows boarded up. But the sidewalks were crowded with men—many of them in militia uniforms Joseph didn't recognize. When he made his way to the front of the group outside the newspaper office, he saw there was nothing posted that he didn't already know:

COUNTY, TOWNS
SEND TROOPS TO CITY
Citizens Rally to Repel
Invasion from North

Disappointed, Joseph made his way back through the crowd to report to the stationmaster. At least it would be fresh news to him.

At the end of the day, Joseph collected his wages and set off for home, the coins jingling in his pocket. He had walked only a block or so when Mr. Kelly caught up to him. "Did you hear?" the man asked. "A mob of secesh are planning to attack Fort McHenry tonight. Probably the same gang that broke into the building where one of the Unionist militia units met. Tell your pa," he called over his shoulder as he hurried on.

Joseph sprinted toward home and was surprised to find Anneliese peeling potatoes when he came in. "They shut down the mill early, Yosef," she said, "and there were notices posted everywhere that the mayor has ordered all the taverns closed."

Pa, who had been dozing in his easy chair by the stove, roused and stretched, and Joseph gave him Mr. Kelly's message about the planned secesh attack on Fort McHenry.

Instantly alert, Pa said, "They are fools! The president cannot lose another fort to southern rebels. If these secesh carry out their plan, Lincoln will send his troops into Baltimore."

Franz clomped down the stairs after sleeping most of the day. "What's this about losing another fort?" he asked. Joseph explained, and Franz said, "Didn't the secesh learn anything from Fort Sumter? Right after the attack, Lincoln called for seventy-five thousand men to put down the rebellion. What do they think he'll do if they try to take McHenry only a week later?"

"Are you going to help protect the fort, Pa?" Erika asked in a small voice.

Pa shook his head. "I will protect my home and family, and I will protect my city, but the soldiers at McHenry must protect their fort without help from me."

"Well, with the reinforcements the government sent to the fort a couple of months ago, they should be prepared for something like this," Franz said. "Besides, a secesh mob—even an armed mob—can't be that much of a threat to the McHenry garrison. Baltimore citizens don't have heavy artillery, you know."

"What I know is that supper is waiting on the table," Ma said. "Come and sit."

Now maybe he could ask Pa about burning the railroad bridges and find out from Franz what went on in the city during the night, Joseph thought. Hearing about it all firsthand would be a lot more exciting than reading the news bulletins.

CHAPTER FIVE

★   ★   ★

JOSEPH HAD just stepped outside the next morning when he heard it again—the clamor of a crowd. Now what? He left his water buckets by the steps and followed the sound toward the harbor. The waterfront was teeming with people. What were they doing here at this hour on a Sunday?

"Great news about the troops, ain't it?" said an excited boy standing at the edge of the crowd.

"Which troops do you mean?" Joseph asked.

"The ones that just arrived on the bay steamer *Louisiana*, of course!"

The old man who was with him said, "Seven hundred of 'em, is what we heard. Seven hundred southern boys come to help protect Baltimore from northern aggression."

"But I don't see any soldiers," the boy said.

"I don't see the *Louisiana*," Joseph said, scanning the vessels moored along the docks, looking carefully at the steamboats scattered among the tall-masted sailing ships.

The old man spat on the ground. "Another rumor, I guess, like last night's attack on McHenry that never happened," he said.

Joseph looked across the water toward the mouth of the harbor, where the high walls of the fort rose from the water's edge. A lump formed in his throat when he saw the huge garrison flag that flew high above it—probably the only U.S. flag for miles around. How did the "star-spangled banner" that had cheered Baltimore's people after the 1814 naval battle become such a hated symbol for so many in the city today?

After one last look at the flag, Joseph made his way through the disappointed crowd milling around the street nearest the harbor. Back home, he picked up the buckets he had abandoned outside the door and set off with them. He was sure that Harold's family had water pumped right into their house—not that Harold would have been the one to fetch it if they didn't.

At church later that morning, Joseph noticed that Pa was one of the only men in the congregation. The few other men and older boys who sat with their families were wearing their militia uniforms, and Joseph figured that the rest were on duty or at their arsenals, as Franz was. *Soon as I'm sixteen, I'll join the militia, too.*

Joseph was daydreaming through mass, imagining himself carrying the flag in the Independence Day parade, when a man on horseback rode up to the open door of the church and hollered, "Yankees from Pennsylvania are marching into Maryland—thousands of 'em!"

The stunned silence in the sanctuary was followed by a rustling sound as the uniformed men and boys made their way to the nearest aisle and then to the door. Joseph's eyes followed them, and he wished he dared slip away to find out more. Near the front of the church, a baby began to fret, and the priest raised his voice and said, "Go to your homes, my children. I will pray for your safety and that of our city."

Even before he finished speaking, the people were on their feet and spilling into the aisles. It was worse than the end of the school day. Almost at once, the scuffle and murmuring of the congregation was drowned out by the ringing of the church bell. By the time Joseph had followed his parents outside, the air was filled with the peals of other bells sounding the alarm.

"That would be a pretty thing to hear if you did not know that it meant trouble," Ma said, leaning her weight on Pa's arm.

The family was slowly making their way toward home when another sound reached Joseph's ears—the beating of drums to call out the militia. "If you want, I'll go find out what's happening," he said, hoping he didn't sound as eager as he felt.

"*You* are the one that wants," Ma grumbled.

"Go and find out, Yosef," Pa said, "but this time, come straight home."

Grateful that Pa had let him go, Joseph dashed off. He could feel his mother's disapproving eyes boring into his back, could sense his little sisters' envy of his freedom, and he wondered if Harold chafed at being with *his* family. Was it different if you were rich, or did his classmates feel this same lightness the minute they were off on their own?

Rounding the next corner, Joseph saw men and older boys rushing toward their armories. He had never seen so much activity in the city on a Sunday, and he wished he could be part of it. If only he were sixteen *now*!

When he came in sight of the newspaper office, he saw that hordes of people were there before him. He shouldered his way toward the building until he could see the bulletin posted outside:

3000 NORTHERN TROOPS
17 MILES FROM CITY!

Joseph's throat went dry. It wasn't much more than what the horseman had shouted into the church during mass, but seeing the words in print somehow gave them greater importance. He stared at the bulletin a moment longer, trying to imagine three thousand soldiers marching on Baltimore, and then he raced for home.

He burst into the house and gasped out what he had learned. Pa broke the silence that followed. "Seventeen miles, you say? Then they are near Cockeysville, and if the railroad bridge there had not been burned, three thousand angry Pennsylvanians would be arriving in our city."

"So now you will go with the others to make sure these men do not march into Baltimore." Ma sounded resigned. "Better that you do not leave until you have had your Sunday dinner." She handed each of the little girls a serving bowl, and Anneliese took the heavy platter of *sauerbraten*.

"I think there is no great rush," Pa said, his eyes on the marinated beef roast his oldest daughter was carrying. "We had many hours of waiting before we left to destroy the railroad bridges."

Frieda took her place opposite Joseph and said, "If Franz was here, he wouldn't wait till after dinner. He'd of gone as soon as he heard the Yankees were coming."

Pa nodded. "Franz finds all this exciting."

It *is* exciting, Joseph thought, passing along the bowl of boiled potatoes. Not knowing what would happen next was scary, but it made him feel—alive.

Pa finished his meal and pushed back his chair. "Well, I go now to join what they are calling the 'un-uniformed volunteers.' Yosef, again you must look after your mother and sisters."

The door had hardly shut behind Pa when Frieda gave Joseph a challenging look and asked, "How will you protect us from the Yankees, Yosef? With your pocketknife?"

"The Yankees will be too busy burning the city to bother with mouthy little girls."

Frieda's eyes widened, and Erika asked, "Will they burn our house, Yosef?"

"You must ignore your brother when he is teasing," Ma said. "And you must learn that most things we worry about do not happen."

"I'll go see if any more bulletins have been posted," Joseph said. "Just so we can be prepared. I can be back in half an hour."

Ma raised her eyes to the ceiling and said, "Go, Yosef. Just go," and he headed for the door.

The sidewalks were even more crowded than they had been earlier, and Joseph sensed an excitement that bordered on panic. At the newspaper office, most of the men stood in clusters, talking about the latest bulletin, though a few stood alone and waited in brooding silence for more news to arrive. Joseph wove his way through the crowd until he could read the most recent headlines:

POLICE CUT
TELEGRAPH LINES
TO NORTH;
CITY CONTROLS
LINES TO SOUTH
SOME VOLUNTEERS
TO BE ARMED
WITH PIKES
Six O'Clock Curfew
Set for Minors

Pa wouldn't much like it if the "un-uniformed volunteers" were given pikes instead of muskets, Joseph thought. He was about to start home when Harold clapped a hand on his shoulder and said, "Isn't it great news about the telegraph lines?" He noticed Joseph's puzzled look and said, "Don't you see? We've got Washington completely cut off from the North—no rail traffic and no news getting through in either direction."

Joseph hadn't thought of that. "Washington's isolated, then," he said as they moved away from the bulletin board. In his mind's eye, he could see the page in his geography book showing the capital city surrounded on three sides by Maryland, with Virginia just across the Potomac River. Angry, rioting Maryland and rebellious, Confederate Virginia. "I sure wouldn't want to be in Abe Lincoln's shoes," Joseph said honestly.

"Once Confederate soldiers march into Washington and capture him and his cabinet, there won't be any question that the South is an independent nation," Harold said. "Maybe *then* the governor will call a convention so Maryland can vote to secede and join the Confederacy."

Joseph didn't answer. He had never dreamed that the rebels might try to capture the president!

"You haven't given me a single reason why Maryland shouldn't join the Confederacy, Joseph—all you ever say is that we'd be better off if we're neutral. I'm beginning to think Alexander's right about you being a Unionist."

"You can think what you want," Joseph said, his voice tense, "but the riot on Friday was a picnic compared to what will happen if we secede. Maryland will be the battle-ground of the war. Don't you see? Northern troops will pour into Maryland and the Confederates will rush here to stop them."

"You don't have to worry about that," Harold scoffed. "One good battle will be enough to make those Yankees decide to move their capital to Philadelphia or New York and let the South go its own way."

Joseph didn't answer. He thought it was obvious that Lincoln had no intention of letting the South go.

"Hey, I was only joking about thinking you were a Unionist," Harold said. "You're not mad, are you?"

"You sounded serious enough to me," Joseph said, surprised to hear the note of concern in Harold's voice. "I'm glad you didn't mean it."

"Of course I didn't. Listen, I've got to get home for Sunday dinner, Joseph. See you at school tomorrow."

I told Ma I'd be home in half an hour. Joseph set off at a run, skirting the crowds gathered outside the armories. But near Pratt Street, he heard a fife and drum, and he stopped to watch a column of militiamen pass. The butcher's small son was marching along beside them, a wooden gun held to his shoulder, and Joseph called, "Hey, Tony! What's going on?"

Without missing a step, the boy called back, "Two more militia units came to help protect the city. They just sailed in on a bay steamer."

But not seven hundred of them, I'll bet. The rhythmic beat of the drum and the high-pitched notes of the fife made Joseph's pulse race as he watched the men march past, the Maryland flag waving above them and sunlight glinting on their bayonets. It was a stirring sight, but the red, black, and gold of the state flag didn't move him the way the red, white, and blue of the Stars and Stripes always had.

Joseph was almost home when an elderly neighbor called from his window and asked in a quavery voice, "Did you see him?"

"See *who*, sir?"

"Jefferson Davis, that's who. The President of the Confederacy. He's on his way here with a hundred thousand southern boys to help us hold off the Yankees."

Somehow, Joseph managed not to laugh. "No, sir. I didn't see him." He ran down the block toward home, aware that his half hour had stretched to at least twice that.

Silence greeted him when he rushed into the house, but by the time he had told about the latest bulletin and described all that he had seen, his sisters were wide-eyed, and his mother was listening with undisguised interest, the tight expression gone from her face.

When he finished, Frieda asked, "Ma, can Yosef take me and Erika to see all the soldiers?"

"Of course not! This is a time for girls and women to stay home."

"It's not fair! Yosef gets to do anything he wants, but we—"

"Don't whine, Frieda," Anneliese said. She looked up from the sock she was darning and added, "That's just the way it is."

Joseph glanced at Frieda to see how she reacted to her older sister's words, and she crossed her eyes at him.

"If you are not careful, your face will freeze like that, young lady," Ma said, just as Joseph had known she would.

"Hey, it would be an improvement," he said. Frieda began to cry, and Erika sent him an accusing look. If Franz had said that, everybody would have laughed, Joseph

67

thought when Anneliese frowned across the table at him and Ma gave an exaggerated sigh. He wondered what Sunday afternoons were like at Harold's house.

Hours later, Joseph was checking over the math problems he'd done Friday morning, half listening to the Bible story Anneliese was telling the younger girls. He glanced up when the front door opened and his brother came in. "Hey, Franz—don't tell me that six o'clock curfew for minors counts for the militia."

"My unit's been dismissed," Franz announced. "You're not going to believe this, but Lincoln has agreed not to send any more troops through Baltimore—and he's telling those Pennsylvanians up at Cockeysville to go back home."

Then the threat to the city is over. But with the rail bridges destroyed, how will Lincoln's volunteers get to Washington?

"I'm starved," Franz said. "Is it long till supper?"

"The girls and I will have it on the table in a few minutes, Franz," Anneliese said, ignoring her sisters' dismay at having their story interrupted. "Don't get up, Ma—stay off that sprained ankle while you can."

"Why do you think Lincoln backed down like that?" Joseph asked his brother, thinking again of what Harold had said about Washington being cut off from the northern states.

"From what I heard, the mayor took the B&O to Washington and convinced the president that it was the only way to calm things down here in Baltimore. And it looks like he was right, too. Soon as people heard the announcement, the crowds in the streets cleared away."

"Then Yosef won't get to stay home from school tomorrow," Erika said, a triumphant look on her face. "It wasn't fair that we had to go on Friday and he didn't."

Ma looked up from her needlework and asked, "And what has made you think life is fair?"

Joseph wished Pa would come home. Erika and Frieda were good as gold when he was here, and Ma wasn't nearly so grumpy.

CHAPTER SIX

AFTER ALL that had happened during the past few days, it seemed strange to be setting off for school as usual on Monday morning. Joseph paused at the corner to look toward Federal Hill, rising green and peaceful across the harbor. But that was all that was peaceful. Here it was, barely a week since Fort Sumter fell, and it seemed as though the entire country was up in arms. As Joseph passed the park, he slowed to watch an officer put a group of volunteers through their paces, then hurried on.

The school yard was less crowded than usual. "Where is everybody this morning?" Joseph asked when he joined a group of classmates.

"I guess some of the older fellows are still with their militia units," one of the boys said. "Did you hear the latest? 'Ape' Lincoln has declared a blockade of all Confederate ports!"

"This could make some businessmen think twice about secession," Charles said. "After all, where would Baltimore be without trade?"

And where would our family be? Franz would soon lose

his job if ships bringing in the huge blocks of ice from New England couldn't reach Baltimore, and Anneliese's factory would have to shut down if raw cotton couldn't be brought in from the South—or bolts of cloth shipped out. And if the rebellion lasted till winter, Pa wouldn't be able to find work at the docks.

"Hey, are you all right, Joseph?" Charles asked. "You look sort of pale."

He gave a quick nod. "I was just thinking about what you said. Wondering how long Baltimore could survive without trade."

Harold said impatiently, "You two aren't thinking clearly. The Union blockade makes it more important than ever for Maryland to join the Confederacy and fight for states' rights—and the sooner the better."

"I agree," said another student who had been listening to their conversation. "The governor should call a convention so our legislators can vote for secession and be done with it."

Joseph felt a knot in his stomach. He'd thought the threat to the city was over when Lincoln told the Pennsylvanians marching toward Baltimore to go back home, when he said that no more troops would be sent through the city. But the real danger wasn't soldiers coming from the North—it lay within Maryland itself, because without a doubt, if the legislators voted on secession, they would decide in favor of it.

The nine o'clock bell rang, and Joseph followed the other boys into the building. But instead of concentrating on his lessons, he brooded on the conversation in the school yard—and on his own stupidity. When the trainloads of troops had passed through the city last week, he'd never imagined something like this would come out of it. All he'd thought of was the excitement of seeing them and the exhilaration of being part of the crowd. Then on the weekend, he'd been almost intoxicated by the sense of urgency that had charged the air. He'd never thought about what it all could mean, never imagined that the city's unrest could affect his family's livelihood.

Joseph was brought back to the present by the schoolmaster's voice. "I take it that you do not know the answer, Mr. Schwartz. Perhaps Mr. Wilson will oblige us." Behind him, Joseph heard Charles give the answer *he* could have given if he'd been paying attention, and he felt his face redden with embarrassment.

In spite of Joseph's efforts to keep his mind on his work, the rest of the day passed in a fog, and on his way home, he forgot all about stopping to see if he could work another couple of hours for the stationmaster. In front of the house, his little sisters were skipping rope, but he scarcely noticed them.

Inside, Ma looked up from her ironing and said, "Home so early, Yosef? You are sick, then, no?" Giving him a closer look, she exclaimed, "You *are* sick!" Setting her flatiron back on the stove she said, "Come, let me feel your forehead."

"I'm not feverish, Ma. Honest, I'm not. But I might lie down for a few minutes." Upstairs, he pulled aside the curtain and looked beyond the roofs of another row of houses to the harbor, with its bay steamers and fishing boats and sailing ships from all over the world. He let the curtain fall back across the window and tried not to imagine the docks as quiet all week long as they were on Sundays.

He was sitting on the edge of the bed, taking off his shoes, when he heard his mother's footsteps on the stairs--limping footsteps. His spirits sank even lower as he thought of the day she'd fallen partway down those stairs with an armload of laundry and sprained her ankle. "You shouldn't have come up, Ma," he said when she reached the landing.

"I would not have to, if you had let me check you for fever when I asked downstairs."

Joseph gritted his teeth and sat still while she laid a hand on his forehead. "I'm fine, Ma."

"You have no fever, but you are not fine," she said, and to his surprise, she sat down beside him on the bed. "I think you have some burden on your mind, son. Are you in trouble for missing school on Friday?"

Joseph shook his head. "Nobody said anything about it."

"So what new rumor has made you like this?"

"It isn't a rumor, it's—" Joseph's shoulders slumped. "President Lincoln has declared a blockade of Confederate ports," he said. "No ships can enter or leave their harbors."

His mother limped to the window and pulled back the curtain. "And so if Maryland secedes . . ." Her voice faded away, and she gazed out over the harbor for what seemed like a long time.

At last Joseph said, "Even if Maryland doesn't secede, we won't be able to trade with the southern states."

Still at the window, his mother said, "Not as many workers will be needed on the docks, then." A moment later she added, "When times are hard in the city, no one builds, and the old paving stones on the streets are not replaced. Our family will not be the only one in the neighborhood that will suffer."

"Well, now you know what got me down," Joseph said. And it was worse than he'd imagined—Pa would be out of a job long before cold weather if there was no work for bricklayers and stonemasons.

Ma was silent for a moment, and then she turned to face Joseph. "Where does your brother keep the money he holds back from his wages?"

How does she know about that? "What do you mean?"

She made an impatient sound. "When I go downstairs, you will find the money Franz has saved. Then you must go to the market and bring back for me a sack of cornmeal and as many pounds of dried beans as you can pay for." At the doorway, she paused. "When you hear bad news, you do not go to your bedroom and lie down. You do what you can to make things a little better."

Smarting from her words, Joseph waited until he heard his mother's halting footsteps on the stairs before he knelt to open the bottom drawer of the bureau. Winter clothes were stored there, and his nose wrinkled at the smell of the dried lavender blossoms Ma had sewed into muslin bags to keep moths away. He found the mitten where his brother hid his savings, put the money in his pocket with the coins he'd earned on Saturday morning, and went downstairs.

"I'm leaving, Ma," he said.

His sisters had come inside, and Frieda complained, "He's *always* going somewhere, Ma, but me and Erika—"

"Enough!" Ma said. "He is going on an errand for me."

Joseph set off toward the market, surprised at how much better he felt. Was it because he was "making things a little better" or because Ma had stuck up for him?

By the time he lugged his purchases back to the house, his sisters were doing their homework at the table and Ma was starting supper. "Write down for me how much you spent, Yosef," she said.

Joseph did as he was told and then handed the paper to his mother. She reached for the pencil and wrote something at the bottom. "Here," she said, handing it back to him, "give this to your brother." He saw that underneath the amount she had signed her name in the ornate script she'd learned as a small girl in Germany.

"I'll put it where he'll be sure to find it," Joseph said. Upstairs, he opened the bureau drawer and slipped the note inside the mitten where the money had been. He hoped Franz would think Ma had discovered his hiding place on her own.

After school the next day, Harold said, "You know those northern troops that camped up at Cockeysville on the weekend? Father told me the city's leaders found out they were short of food, and yesterday they sent a couple of wagon loads of meat and bread up there for them! Can you imagine feeding your enemies like that?"

"As long as we're still in the Union, they aren't our enemies," Joseph pointed out, wishing ordinary citizens would show the same decency their leaders did.

"All the more reason for the governor to call a special session of the General Assembly so our legislators can vote to secede," Alexander said. "Or do you still think Maryland ought to be neutral?"

Joseph heard the challenge in the other boy's voice. "It doesn't matter what I think," he said. "If there's a vote, it will be for secession. Everybody knows the secessionists have a majority in the legislature."

Dropping the subject, Alexander said, "Come on, let's go to the sweet shop."

Joseph said, "Count me out. I'm going to see if any more news bulletins have gone up." Why hadn't anyone realized that by cutting the telegraph lines to the north, they were cutting off the news coming into Baltimore as well as the news going to Washington?

"I'll go with you," Harold said. "I'd like to see if there's anything about the Fort McHenry garrison planning to fire on the city."

"Where did you hear that?" Joseph asked as they set off.

"From my cousin."

Young Paul Revere, Joseph thought. He doubted that the story was true, but it wasn't worth arguing about.

Especially when Harold had just chosen his company over Alexander's.

"Randall says the Yankees at the fort have their cannon pointed toward Monument Square, and every one of 'em's aimed right smack at George Washington's statue," Harold announced. "It wouldn't make much sense for Union soldiers to destroy a statue of George Washington, would it?" Joseph asked, realizing that Harold was waiting for his response.

Instead of answering, Harold said, "Hey, look! They're posting a bulletin now." He set off for the newspaper office at a run, with Joseph at his heels.

NORTHERN PRESS
URGES LINCOLN
TO KEEP MARYLAND
IN UNION AT ALL COSTS
Calls for Occupation
Of Baltimore Increase

The words in the last two lines made Joseph's spine tingle. He called to the printer's apprentice, a boy from his neighborhood. "How did that news get through, Karl? I thought the telegraph lines to the north were cut."

Karl paused in the doorway and said, "The magazine dealer down the street had a fellow ride up to one of the towns near the Pennsylvania border and bring back copies of the northern papers."

At least if the Union occupied Maryland, the harbor

would stay open and—

"Now do you believe that the troops at Fort McHenry have their artillery trained on the city?" Harold demanded, breaking into Joseph's thoughts. "They could fire those cannon anytime they want and claim they were just making sure Maryland stayed in the Union."

"I don't know what to believe," Joseph said.

Harold gave him an exasperated look and said, "Well, while you think it over, I'm going to find Randall and tell him about those headlines so he can spread the word. We've got to be prepared!"

The next morning when Joseph arrived at school, he saw a group of boys standing on the front steps of the building. He hurried over in time to hear the end of what Harold was saying: ". . . so now that they've taken over Annapolis, they can control the Chesapeake Bay. And *that* means Baltimore is cut off from the South."

"What's happened?" Joseph asked Charles, who was standing a little apart from the others.

"Some general from Massachusetts brought his troops into Maryland by rail and then commandeered a ferryboat to take them down the bay to Annapolis. They've occupied the city."

Maryland's capital, occupied?

One of the other boys turned to Joseph and added, "And that's not all. They've repaired the rail line the secessionists had torn up between Annapolis and Washington, and that means Lincoln's troops can get to the Union capital without coming through Baltimore."

Alexander said, "Now *we're* cut off. Where do all our roads lead? To Washington, Pennsylvania, and Annapolis. The first two are Yankee territory, and now that the Union's taken Annapolis—"

"They control the Chesapeake," Joseph said, repeating what Harold had just said. The bay was what mattered, the bay and its harbor here in Baltimore. His family's livelihood depended on ships that sailed up the Chesapeake, and because of that, keeping Maryland in the Union mattered as much for practical reasons as for patriotic ones—the city had to be assured of trade with the northern states. Joseph didn't want to think about a Confederate Maryland under a Union naval blockade. About the Schwartz family with no source of income.

"Bean soup, *again*?" Erika complained that evening. "This is the third time in a week."

Before Ma could scold her, Joseph said, "You'd better be glad Ma stocked up on dried beans, Erika, 'cause there's not much to buy at the market. I guess a lot of the farmers are afraid to come into town and set up their stands for fear of trouble."

Ma said, "The vegetable man's wagon has not come to this neighborhood since before the riot, so I have no more cabbage or potatoes. Not even a carrot."

"I hope the secesh are satisfied with what they've done," Frieda said.

"I hope they like bean soup," Erika said, pushing away her bowl.

Franz said, "Those rich secesh are probably eating

baked ham and sweet potato dinners—or maybe codfish and potatoes with apple pie for dessert. You should see the pantries in some of the houses on my ice route."

Pa said, "I think the rich will begin to suffer a little. With not many ships coming into Baltimore now, men have lost their jobs on the docks, and the landlords will hurt some when these men cannot pay their rent."

"Those rich landlords ought to suffer—as long as they still pay their ice bill," Franz said.

At a lull in the conversation, Joseph took a deep breath and said, "Pa, a boy in my class has asked if I want to go to Frederick with him and his father to see the legislature in session on Saturday. His father can get rail passes, so we'll all ride free."

Before Pa could answer, Frieda wailed, "It's not fair! Yosef is always the one that gets to go places!"

"He is the one the boy invited," Pa said mildly.

"And who is this boy from class?" Ma asked. "You have not brought him here to meet your family."

Joseph's heart sank. He'd give up the chance for a day's outing with Harold before he'd bring him here! "His name's Harold Porter, Ma. The boys at the academy are too busy studying to see each other outside of school."

"Except for this trip on Saturday, I take it," Ma said.

Pa's face had a distant look. "I have heard that you can see the mountains from Frederick town," he said.

He's going to let me go! "We might even be there for the vote on secession," Joseph said, excitement creeping into his voice.

Frieda looked puzzled. "At school, we learned that the General Assembly meets in Annapolis."

"That's right," Joseph said, "but with the Union Army controlling the city, the governor decided it would be better if the legislature met somewhere else."

"Our foreman says the governor wants the meeting in a place that is not full of the secesh," Pa said. "I hear that Annapolis is strongly for the South."

Ma said grudgingly, "I will wash and iron your Sunday shirt so you look presentable, Yosef."

"Thanks, Ma." He could hardly believe his luck! He wasn't sure which was the greatest surprise—that of all the boys in the class, Harold had invited him, or that he was being allowed to go.

CHAPTER SEVEN

ON SATURDAY, Joseph arrived at Camden Station long before time to meet Harold and his father. The station was almost deserted at this hour—quite a contrast to the week before, when it had swarmed with rioters and police.

Joseph spotted a bench and headed toward it. Someone had left a newspaper behind—a New York paper! *Maybe now I can find out what's going on in the North.* He set down the package that Ma had insisted he bring—*Zimtplätzchen* she had baked—on the bench beside him, sliding it away so he could conveniently "forget" it. Harold and his father were probably used to eating fancy pastries from a bakery and would think it strange if they knew he'd brought along homemade cookies.

Trying to forget how late Ma had stayed up to bake "something to thank your friend and his father for taking you on the trip," Joseph unfolded the newspaper. The first thing his eyes fell on was an article about the ceremony in honor of the Fort Sumter garrison: "The shot-torn flag that flew over Fort Sumter during the bombardment waved from the statue of George Washington in Union Square today as 100,000 New Yorkers honored the brave men who had defended it and shouted their demands for vengeance against the South."

Joseph stared at the words until they became a blur. *If Maryland's legislators vote to secede, then we'll be part of the South. And we'll be the first state to feel the North's vengeance.* He quickly turned to the editorial pages and was still reading when Harold clapped him on the shoulder.

"Hey, Joseph! Father's letting us go to Frederick without him. He has to deal with some emergency at the office. Come on—I've got our passes."

Joseph noticed a paper-wrapped package under Harold's arm. "What's that you've brought?" he asked.

"Sandwiches, so we won't have to waste time buying a meal in Frederick. I see that you brought something, too."

"Just some cookies," Joseph said. He picked up the *Zimtplätzchen* but left the northern paper behind, even though he hadn't finished it.

A few minutes later, the boys had taken their seats in one of the cars, and Joseph was trying to act as if traveling by rail were an everyday experience. Three young men carrying carpetbags passed them, and Harold whispered, "Probably on their way to Harper's Ferry to join a Virginia regiment. My cousin Randall says that's what he'll do if the legislature doesn't vote for secession."

The whistle blasted, and with a lurch, the train began to move, gradually picking up speed. It was much faster than the street railway—noisier and dirtier, too, Joseph thought as ash from the engine's smokestack blew in through the windows. What an adventure!

West of the city, they rode through gently rolling coun-tryside. Joseph had never seen so much land without buildings on it—and he'd never imagined moving at such a speed. "How fast do you think we're going?" he asked, his eyes on the telegraph lines that seemed to swoop past alongside the tracks.

"I dunno. Maybe twenty-five miles an hour."

Joseph was impressed. That meant the trip to Frederick would take less than two hours! He had begun to feel like an old hand at rail travel when suddenly the land seemed to fall away. Joseph caught his breath and leaned closer to the window. Far below he saw the gleam of water—and nothing else.

"Don't look down, or you'll feel giddy," Harold said, adding, "I hate railroad bridges. Say, why don't we have an early lunch?"

The boys made short work of Harold's ham sandwiches and hard-boiled eggs, and then Joseph unwrapped Ma's package.

"What kind of cookies are these?" Harold asked, help-ing himself.

"They're called *Zimtplätzchen*."

"Sounds German."

I should have just said "cinnamon cookies."

"Mmm." Harold helped himself to several more. "You never mentioned that you had a German cook. What else does she serve you?"

"Oh, things like *sauerbraten*—that's made with becf—

and red cabbage cooked with apples. We all like her sausage and sauerkraut, too."

"You're lucky. Our cook just fixes ordinary food."

Joseph had never imagined that the meals Ma served would make a boy like Harold envious. "Go ahead and finish up the cookies," he said, turning his attention to the window again. He hoped Ma never found out he'd let his new friend think her prized *Zimtplätzchen* had been baked by their "cook." She'd think he was ashamed of his family's German heritage, and he wasn't. But it was just one more thing that set him apart from his classmates.

It didn't make sense, Joseph thought. Most of the recent arrivals to America were for the Union—to them, the word *united* in "these United States" meant just that. It was people like Harold and Alexander, people whose ancestors had been among America's earliest settlers, who were shouting "Down with the United States!" Joseph glanced at Harold, who was brushing cookie crumbs from his lap. *He'd better be glad the U.S. Constitution guarantees free speech. In a lot of countries, people are thrown in jail for speaking out the way he does.*

At last the train began to slow, and Harold said, "Well, here we are. Frederick." He led the way to the door.

"I thought the station would be bigger," Joseph said, glancing around.

"Frederick isn't an important city like Baltimore, don't forget," Harold said. He asked directions to the court house, where the General Assembly was meeting, and the two boys set off.

As they crossed the street, Joseph said, "There sure are a lot of militiamen around the station. And look—more of them are on the next corner. You think they expect some kind of trouble?"

"I think they *are* some kind of trouble," Harold answered. "I don't like the looks of this."

Joseph knew that from Frederick on west, Maryland was mostly Unionist, but that didn't explain all the uniformed men. Still, he was too busy looking at the nearby mountains to worry about it. Federal Hill was nothing compared to the tree-covered slopes that seemed to lie just beyond the town or the soft blue of the mountains rising in the distance.

Before they'd gone very far, Harold said, "That ought to be the court house just ahead."

They had almost reached the door when a militiaman called, "The court house is closed, boys."

"Isn't this where the legislature's meeting?" Harold asked.

"Not anymore," the man said. "It was too crowded here, so they've moved to the building at the corner of Market and East Church Street."

Joseph looked in the direction the man pointed and saw a crowd gathered on the sidewalk in front of a large three-story building.

"Did they vote on secession yet?" Harold asked eagerly.

The militiaman shook his head. "Nope. And they're not going to, either. I don't know about the House of Delegates, but the senators already decided they had no authority to vote on secession issues."

"They decided *what*?" the boys asked in unison.

The man grinned and said, "You heard me. The vote was unanimous."

Joseph was speechless with relief, but Harold laughed and said, "For a minute there, you had us fooled, mister."

The militiaman rocked back on his heels and said, "I'm telling you the honest truth. So if you've come here hoping to watch Maryland vote itself out of the Union, you might as well go on back to Baltimore."

"How did you know that's where we're from?" Joseph demanded.

"'Cause the two of you look like secesh. Now move along."

Joseph didn't have to be told twice. Smarting from being told he "looked like secesh," he turned toward the building where the Assembly was now meeting, but he'd taken only a step or two when the man bellowed, "Not that way, boy—back to the station. We don't want your lot here."

Without a word, Joseph turned and retraced his steps. He walked silently beside Harold, who didn't stop cursing the Union until they were almost to the next corner, where two militiamen stood guard.

After they crossed the street, Harold pulled a folded schedule from his pocket and studied it. "If we hurry, we can catch the next train home. Come on—being around all these Unionists makes me want to puke."

Somehow, Joseph managed not to let his expression

change. He'd have to be more careful than ever about what he said. Now that he'd finally made a friend, he didn't want to lose him.

Neither boy spoke until they were seated in the Gentlemen's Parlor of the small station, waiting for their train to arrive. "I still can't believe every single one of our senators voted not to even discuss secession," Harold said.

A middle-aged man with a secession badge on his lapel looked up from his newspaper. "You don't realize what they were up against," he said. "What would *you* have done if members of the Home Guard threatened to drive you out the window of the Senate chamber at the point of a bayonet if you dared to vote for secession?"

Without waiting for an answer, he gestured to a trio of uniformed men just outside the door and said, "The Home Guard has taken it upon themselves to make sure Maryland stays in the Union, and they don't care how they do it. They patrol the streets day and night, and from what I hear, they're keeping an eye on the legislators as well as any strangers that are in town. Wouldn't let me anywhere near a member of the General Assembly."

"They wouldn't even let us near the building where they were meeting," Harold said.

The train's whistle announced its approach from the west, and the man headed for the platform, leaving his *Richmond Times* behind. Joseph would have liked to read it on the way home, but he was concerned that Harold might think it crass to pick up something that had been discarded.

The train braked to a stop in a cloud of steam, and the boys climbed on. Harold slumped into a seat and said, "What a wasted day. Wake me up when we get back."

It might have been a wasted day for Harold, but it was an exciting one for me, Joseph thought. The train trip, watching the countryside flash past the window, seeing the mountains, finding out that there would be no vote in favor of secession—it was the best day I've ever had, in spite of being told I "look like secesh."

At the supper table that evening, Joseph told everything he could remember about the trip to Frederick, ending by saying, "Harold really enjoyed your *Zimtplätzchen*, Ma."

"And you did not want to take it with you. You thought it was something not good enough for your rich friend."

How did she know? Joseph was glad when his brother spoke.

"I heard something interesting when I was on my rounds today," Franz said. "It seems that a couple of the legislators who favored secession were 'persuaded' to stay away from the Assembly session."

Anneliese's brow creased. "But who persuaded them?"

"Unionist militiamen. The hired girl at a place where I delivered ice this morning said the man of the house was stopped by a group of 'em when he got off the train in Frederick. Soon as they saw the red and white cockade he was wearing, they convinced him to take the next train back to Baltimore."

Pa's eyebrows rose. "How can this be true? People come to America because they hear that such things do not happen here. Because the Constitution protects against it."

"Maybe so, but on my way home today, I heard a newspaper boy calling out something about President Lincoln suspending people's rights," Franz said.

"Something about 'suspending the writ of habeas corpus'?" Joseph asked.

Franz's eyes brightened. "That was it!" he said.

"What on earth does it mean?" Anneliese asked.

Joseph said, "It's Latin, and it means the government can arrest somebody without telling them why. Without even having a reason."

After a moment of shocked silence, Ma said, "Are you telling us that Abraham Lincoln will let people go to jail without a trial? How can that happen in America?"

"Because of the South's rebellion, I think," Joseph told her, trying to remember what he'd learned when his class had studied the Constitution.

In a small voice Erika asked, "Will they arrest Pa?"

"Of course not," Joseph said. "They'll only arrest the secesh." The panicky look left his sister's eyes, and Joseph half wished that he could be eight years old again.

CHAPTER EIGHT

ON MONDAY, Joseph was surprised to see Charles at the center of a cluster of boys in the school yard, but then he realized that it was the newspaper Charles had brought that interested his classmates.

Noticing Joseph on the edge of the group, Charles held up the paper so he could read the headline: **ARREST OF MARYLAND LEGISLATURE.**

"That headline is a bit misleading," Charles said, and he read from the article, "'General Butler, commanding at Annapolis, says that if the Maryland legislature presses an ordinance of secession, he will arrest the entire body.'"

Joseph was speechless, but Harold turned to him and said, "I guess now we know why our senators decided they didn't have the authority to vote on the secession issue."

"I keep telling you, that general is talking through his hat. He can't arrest anybody, much less the whole legislature," another boy argued.

"Actually, he can," Joseph said. "Now that Lincoln's suspended the writ of habeas corpus, military authorities can arrest whoever they want to."

One of his classmates said scornfully, "I don't see why

anyone would want to stay in Lincoln's precious Union if he's taking away their Constitutional rights."

"He didn't suspend the writ everywhere," Joseph reminded him, "just here in Maryland."

"And not everywhere in Maryland," Charles added. "Just 'along a line between Washington and Philadelphia,' according to the newspaper."

His eyes blazing, Harold said, "It's no coincidence that the line goes through the part of the state where people have southern sympathies. Lincoln's taking away the rights of people who might not vote the way he wants them to on the secession issue. Some democracy."

Joseph was glad the bell rang and ended the conversation. It was hard always to be on guard so he didn't say something that showed his Unionist sympathies, like pointing out that the Washington-to-Philadelphia line sounded like the route of the railroad and telegraph, and the president would be foolish not to protect them.

By afternoon, the late April day was so warm the classroom felt stuffy even though the windows were wide open. The Latin teacher droned on, and in spite of Joseph's best intentions, his mind drifted away from the lesson. It was almost as if the riot had never happened, he thought. Less than two weeks ago, the city had been in chaos, and already the telegraph lines had been repaired and the railroad bridges were being rebuilt. Coming back from the noon break, he'd heard a rumor that now the lower house of the legislature as well as the Senate had voted against bringing up the subject of secession, and he hoped it was true.

Joseph was relieved when the Latin master dismissed the class and school was out for the day. He was gathering his books together when Harold paused by his desk and said, "Let's go buy a newspaper and find out what's going on."

They hadn't walked far before they heard a newsboy calling out, "Extra! Extra! Maryland legislature—"

Harold swore when the rest of the sentence was drowned out by the clatter of hooves and creak of wagon wheels. "Come on," he called, sprinting toward the corner.

Several men were clustered around the newsboy, and when Joseph and Harold ran up, the boy said, "Sorry— just sold the last one." A young man who looked as though he might be a clerk held his paper so they could read the headline:

MARYLAND LEGISLATURE
VOTES AGAINST SECESSION

Joseph felt a sense of relief, but Harold's shoulders slumped. "I was sure we'd leave the Union," he said, his voice flat.

"So was I," Joseph said honestly, "until we went to Frederick on Saturday." *Now ships from the North will be allowed to sail up the Chesapeake to Baltimore. The docks will be busy again, and the ice plant and factories will stay open. We'll be able to buy what we need.* "I'd better get on home with the news," he said. Ma would be relieved to hear it.

"I'll have to see if Randall knows yet. He said that if this happened, his whole militia unit would take the B&O to Harper's Ferry, Virginia, and enlist in the Confederate Army."

Maybe Pa was right that one reason the city's been quiet lately is that a lot of secesh have gone south, Joseph thought. "Well, see you tomorrow, then," he said, wondering what would happen next.

"Hey, come look at the badges Alexander brought," one of the boys called, gesturing for Joseph to join them under a tree in the school yard on Thursday morning.

Joseph wasn't surprised when he saw the three broad bars—red, white, red—and circle of stars on a blue field. Confederate flag badges.

"Go on and take one, Joe," Alexander urged. "I've got plenty."

"You know very well that I'm not a secessionist," Joseph said.

Alexander turned to Harold and said, "What did I tell you? I'm surprised he isn't wearing the Stars and Stripes."

"How come you don't have a badge of the Maryland flag?" Joseph asked. "I'd wear one of those."

"If you're so strong for Maryland, you must be for states' rights," one of the boys said, looking puzzled. "But if you're for states' rights, I don't see why you're neutral instead of for the Confederacy."

Alexander gave Joseph a scornful glance and said, "Aw, he's just afraid to take a stand."

It was true, but Joseph hated hearing it. He grabbed the front of Alexander's shirt and pulled him forward until their faces were inches apart. "You take that back, Alex. Or else."

"Lay off! You know I didn't mean anything by that, Joe!"

Alexander doesn't want to fight me. A feeling of power surged through Joseph. "Then take it back," he said, tightening his grip.

"Let go of me—I take it back!"

"Say it, then," Joseph demanded.

"You're not afraid to take a stand!" Alexander gasped out.

Joseph shoved him away. "Make sure you remember that," he said in the menacing tone he'd heard Franz use with a neighborhood bully. He watched Alexander stoop to pick up the badges that had scattered on the ground, noticed that Harold didn't help, and wished he'd put Alexander in his place sooner. "And another thing, Alex— don't call me 'Joe.'"

The school bell rang, and the boys who had gathered with the hope of seeing a fight moved toward the building. Joseph followed them, and when Charles held the door for him, Joseph noticed that he wasn't wearing one of Alexander's badges, either. "Thanks, Charles," he said, but the other boy was already hurrying down the hall.

After school a few days later, Joseph and Harold set off to check the bulletin board at the newspaper office, as they did each day now. Joseph had noticed that ever since the riot, Harold had been spending more time with him and less with Alexander, and he was glad of it. It bothered him, though, that he couldn't be honest about being a Unionist. He'd never actually lied about it, but he *had* deliberately misled Harold, and now that they were friends, he felt guilty.

As soon as they saw the knots of men deep in conversation outside the newspaper office, the boys walked faster. "Whatever the news is, they don't look happy about it," Joseph said. He figured that was a safe enough observation—he'd gotten pretty good at making comments that were true but wouldn't give him away. Still, he was glad Pa didn't know how carefully he walked the thin line between truth and falsehood. Pa would be ashamed of him—and Ma would be disgusted. *But they don't understand.*

When they were close enough to read the bulletin, Harold swore under his breath.

UNION TROOPS STOP TRAINS
ON B&O LINE WEST OF CITY;
CARS SEARCHED FOR GOODS
EN ROUTE TO CONFEDERATES
AT HARPER'S FERRY

"It's a good thing Cousin Randall and the other fellows in his militia unit already left for Virginia to join the Confederate army. Can you imagine how they'd react to having the Yankees stop their train?"

"I sure can," Joseph said, remembering how ordinary citizens had reacted when northern troops simply passed through the city. "And I wouldn't like it any better than they would." Wasn't this supposed to be the land of the free?

An old man who had witnessed their reaction to the news said, "Those Federal troops are in a position to intimidate our legislators in Frederick now. They're General Butler's men, you know."

"Wait a minute," Harold said. "Isn't Butler the one who threatened to arrest the whole legislature if they changed their mind and voted on secession? The one who occupied Annapolis and opened the rail line to Washington?"

The man nodded. "The very one. And he commands the Sixth Massachusetts—the regiment that was caught up in the Pratt Street riot last month."

A shiver ran up Joseph's spine. "Sounds like they're in a position to intimidate Baltimore as well as the legislature," he said.

The door to the newspaper office opened, and everyone crowded around to read the new bulletin as soon as the apprentice posted it:

REPAIRS ON BURNED BRIDGES
NEAR COMPLETION;
RAIL LINES FROM NORTH
TO OPEN TOMORROW

"I guess with General Butler's men so close to the city,

Lincoln's volunteers don't have to worry about crossing town on their way to Camden Station," Joseph said. Now there would be a lot more than a handful of citizens killed if anyone started trouble.

Harold nodded. "I guess we've had our fun," he said. "Well, see you tomorrow."

"See you tomorrow," Joseph echoed. He watched his friend head toward home, wondering how he could think the riot had been fun.

At supper the next evening, Anneliese announced, "The newsboys were crying out something about how Mayor Brown and the city council announced that the people must submit to the federal government. I wish I knew what it all means."

"It means that Baltimore citizens must behave like Americans and support their president even though they didn't vote for him," Pa said.

"But what if they don't?" Frieda asked. "What if people think the southern states have the right to set up their own country?"

Pa turned to her and said shortly, "Then they should go to live in the southern states." When he saw the little girl wilt, his voice softened, and he said, "This country has been good to us, *Liebchen*, and we must support it. All the states united is better than groups of rival states, as we had for so long in our old homeland."

"Still, I do not like the idea of boys like Jonathan from Pennsylvania leaving home to put down this rebellion in the South," Ma said, passing a bowl of sauerkraut to Franz.

"Jonathan and the others will be giving only three months to their country," Pa said. "That is all the president has asked of them."

Joseph said, "But now the president has called for men to sign up to serve for three *years*. I saw the bulletin just a few days ago."

After a shocked silence, Ma asked, "And how many more will he ask for when another week passes? I think Mr. Lincoln's 'rebellion' is becoming a war."

A civil war, Joseph thought. The worst kind. But at least Maryland won't be its battleground. Since we aren't leaving the Union, Virginia will be the northernmost of the Confederate states. He glanced across the table at Franz, who was scowling down at his plate. *I'll bet Franz is wishing he could walk into one of the recruiting stations and sign on to fight for the Union. But three years is a long time.*

CHAPTER NINE

JOSEPH STOPPED short when he saw the U.S. flag flying high above Federal Hill on Monday morning—and cannon barrels pointed toward downtown. He raced back home, the empty water buckets banging against his legs.

"The city's been taken over by Union troops!" he shouted. "Baltimore's been *occupied*!"

Franz scowled and said, "I didn't like it last week when that Union general took over the B&O rail line to the west, but this is even worse. Makes you wonder what they might do next."

Before anyone could speculate about that, Frieda asked, "How come you brought back empty buckets, Yosef? Don't you know Ma needs to heat water so Erika and I can wash the dishes after breakfast?"

"News will keep, Yosef," Ma said, "but your sisters must go to school on time."

Without a word, Joseph picked up the buckets and left the house.

On his way to the academy nearly an hour later, he sensed that something was different. It took several minutes before he figured out what it was: No Confederate flags were flying, and no militiamen were in sight. Without militia units drilling, the city seemed strangely quiet.

Ahead of him, several men had gathered to read a sign nailed to a tree, and Joseph ran to join them. They moved over to make room for him, and one of them said, "It's a proclamation from the Yankee general over on Federal Hill."

"So *that's* why there aren't any flags!" Joseph exclaimed when he came to the part that prohibited flying the Confederate colors. Maybe now the Unionists would bring out the U.S. flags they'd taken down the day of the riot, he thought, suddenly aware of how much he'd missed seeing the Stars and Stripes. He considered detouring past the newspaper office to read the bulletins about the occupation but decided there wasn't time for that.

The first thing Joseph noticed when he arrived in the school yard was his classmates' grim faces, and then he saw that the flag badges Alexander had passed out had disappeared from their jackets.

"So you know about the occupation," Joseph said.

Everyone nodded, and several of the boys muttered, "We know." The bell rang, and as they headed slowly toward the building, Joseph matched his pace to theirs.

When he turned into the school yard after the noon break, Joseph immediately noticed a change in his classmates, and as he walked toward them, he sensed an undercurrent of excitement—or maybe anger.

Harold turned to him, his eyes blazing. "Did you hear about Ross Winans?"

"What about him?" Joseph asked, wondering if Harold

knew the rich industrialist and legislator personally.

"The Yankees have arrested him! They're holding him prisoner at Fort McHenry!"

Joseph's eyes widened. "But *why*?"

"For being a Confederate, that's why," one of his classmates said at the same time Harold said, "For his 'secessionist activities.' He gave a lot of money to our cause—and weapons, too."

"I can't believe the president ever intended for an old man like Mr. Winans to be thrown into prison!" Joseph exclaimed.

Alexander turned to Harold and said, "Listen to him—'the president'! I *told* you he was a Unionist. He's no more neutral than you and me."

Harold looked at Joseph. "Is he right? *Are* you a Unionist?"

Joseph's heart sank. "Yes, but—"

"I knew it!" Alexander said triumphantly. "He sure pulled the wool over your eyes, Harold."

Harold's face flushed and he took a step toward Joseph. "You coward. You lying coward. Alexander was right about you being afraid to take a stand."

Joseph was stunned. What could he say that wouldn't make things worse than they already were?

"Lying Unionist coward," Alexander taunted, and other boys gathered around, taking up the chant.

The look of satisfaction and sly superiority on Alexander's face was more than Joseph could take. He stepped toward the other boy and began to roll up his sleeves. "You'll wish you hadn't said that, Alex." The flicker of fear in the other boy's eyes almost made him smile. He'd show these rich secessionists who the coward was!

But Harold forced his way between them and said, "Leave Alex alone. What he said is true—you're a lying Unionist coward."

Joseph's fist swung upward and smashed into Harold's chin with such force that the other boy staggered backward into Alexander, almost knocking him off balance. Breathing hard, Joseph waited, his eyes on Harold but keenly aware of the sullen murmur from the circle of boys who had gathered to watch. *How did this happen? I wanted to fight Alex, not Harold.*

The school bell rang, and the other boys began to move toward the door—except for Harold. One hand on his jaw, he faced Joseph and asked, "Why did you do it?"

Why did he think I did it? "Because of what you said."

"Not why did you hit me—why did you lie about what you believed?"

The mixture of hurt and scorn in Harold's expression made Joseph drop his gaze, and he stared at the ground until Harold walked away. Then, following him with his eyes, Joseph answered silently, Because I wanted to fit in here at school. Because I wanted you to be my friend.

That was the truth of it, but it wasn't something he could admit to. "I was stupid," Joseph whispered as he walked away from the school yard. Stupid to think that a working-class boy could fit in with rich men's sons. Stupid to pretend to be someone I wasn't. And just plain wrong to let Harold think Ma was our German cook. I'll make it up to her. If I ever make another friend, I'll take him home to meet her. I'll ask her to bake *Zimtplätzchen* for us. I'll go to confession and do whatever penance the priest gives me, and maybe then—

"Hey, Joseph!"

Jolted out of his reverie, Joseph turned to see Franz waving from the seat of his ice wagon. "I see you're playing hooky," Franz said when he had brought his horse to a stop near the curb.

Joseph climbed to the wagon seat beside him and asked, "Can I drive?"

"Why not? Nelly knows the route." Franz handed over the reins, and the brothers rode in silence until he announced, "I've told the boss I'm quitting at the end of the week."

Joseph stared at him. "But I thought you liked your job! Have you found one that pays more, then?"

After they rattled across the tracks of the street railway, Franz said, "I'm going to join the army, Yosef."

Half excited, half dismayed, Joseph asked, "Can I come along when you go to the recruiting office to volunteer? Just to see what it's like?"

Franz took the reins to guide the wagon between a delivery wagon and a street vendor's cart, then handed them back. Without looking at Joseph, he said, "I won't be going to the Union recruiting office downtown. I'll be volunteering in Virginia."

"In *Virginia*? You're joining the *rebel* army?"

Franz nodded. "I believed in the Union just as much as

you do, Yosef. Just as much as Pa does. All that business about the rule of law and upholding the Constitution, all those safeguards we were guaranteed in the Bill of Rights. But look what's happened—Marylanders are being thrown in jail without a trial, and soldiers have occupied Baltimore."

"We've been occupied to make sure the rail lines and telegraph lines from Washington to the north are kept open," Joseph said. "They've already been cut once, if you remember."

"Maybe so, but I'm going to fight on the side of freedom," Franz said, and Joseph saw that his brother's face had the same closed, stubborn expression it had worn years ago whenever Ma scolded him. "I know Pa won't like it," Franz went on, "but he'll understand. After all, he's the one who taught us to stand up for what we believe in."

I didn't even admit to what I believe in, much less stand up for it, and Pa will never understand that. "What about Ma? She won't want you to do this."

"I know. But she can't stop me."

"How will you get to Virginia now that the Union controls the railroad between here and Harper's Ferry?" Joseph asked.

"Don't you worry about that," Franz said. "I've already figured out a way."

But he isn't going to tell me because I'm a Unionist. In less than an hour, I've lost my friend and my brother. Joseph blinked back tears, hoping Franz wouldn't notice.

"You haven't said why you're not in school," his brother reminded him.

Joseph told him, adding, "So because I'm for the Union, all the boys at school are against me, and my own brother doesn't trust me enough to tell me how he's getting to Virginia."

"After I collect my pay on Friday, I'll hitch a ride out of town with the vegetable man," Franz said. "His youngest son and I will make our way to Virginia together."

Franz *did* trust him. "Maybe I could ride along with you like this for the rest of the week," Joseph said.

The horse stopped in front of a large brick house, and before Franz climbed down from the wagon seat, he gave Joseph a long look. "If you don't go back and finish out the school year, you'll prove Alexander was right when he called you a coward. And don't take the easy way out by showing up late, you hear?"

Joseph nodded. He stared down at the schoolbooks on his lap and told himself he could take anything for the few days until the term ended. He'd managed a lot longer than that without friends at the beginning of the year, after all. But then it was because he didn't know anyone, and now it would be because of what everyone knew about him.

Joseph was still several blocks from school the next morning when he saw Harold walking toward him. *What's going on? Why is he coming to meet me?* When they were only a few feet apart, they both stopped, and Joseph waited for the other boy to speak.

"Alex has got a bunch of the fellows ready to jump you the minute you walk into the school yard," Harold said.

"You'd better not show up until after the bell rings."

"How come you're warning me?"

Harold shrugged. "We were friends. I don't want to see you beat up."

Were friends. "Thanks, but I'd better face them. Otherwise, they'll just lie in wait for me at noon, or maybe after school. How many do you think they are?"

"Five, maybe six," Harold said, falling into step beside Joseph.

Joseph's stomach tightened. "I'll just have to hope they don't do too much damage before the bell rings." After a few more steps he added, "Look, I'm sorry I punched you yesterday, Harold."

"Forget it. I shouldn't have said what I did."

He shouldn't have said it, but he's not sorry. He isn't going to take it back. Joseph had never felt more miser able. A block from the school, he glanced at Harold and said, "You'd better let me go on ahead so Alex and the others don't see us together."

"Are you crazy? I'm not letting you face them alone!"

Harold is going to stand by me! They were almost to the edge of the school yard when a group of boys who had been sitting on the steps stood up. A lot more than six of them, Joseph saw, his courage faltering. Alexander yelled, "Grab him, Harold! Hold him so he can't run away." He swaggered toward Joseph, glancing back to make sure the others were following him.

"He won't run," Harold called. "He's going to fight you—and I'm going to help him."

Alexander's steps faltered, and he stopped a few feet away. "You are? *Why*?"

"Because ganging up on him like you've planned is unworthy of southern gentlemen."

If Joseph hadn't been so scared, he would have laughed. Unworthy of southern gentlemen? But Harold's words seemed to affect the others. One of the boys said, "He's right, Alex," and another said, "Count me out." Shamefaced, they all turned away.

"If you want to fight, I'll be glad to oblige," Joseph said. "Might as well settle things between us once and for all." He slipped his book strap off his shoulder and lowered his schoolbooks to the ground. He was shrugging out of his jacket when Alexander took a step back.

"I'm not wasting my time on the likes of you—*Joe*."

As Joseph watched Alexander head toward the building, Harold asked, "Why is that ice wagon parked across the street? The driver seems to be looking this way."

Joseph glanced over his shoulder in time to see Franz slap the reins on Nelly's back. His brother had come to help him out if there was a fight! Should he tell Harold that the driver of the ice wagon was his brother? No, the time to be straightforward was long past, and besides, Harold was already walking toward the building with two of the boys who hadn't taken part in Alexander's plan.

So that's the way it's going to be, Joseph thought. Harold stuck up for me because it was the gentlemanly thing to do even though our friendship is over—and it's over not because I'm a Unionist, but because I deceived him. Because

I didn't take a stand. No wonder Harold doesn't think much of me. I don't think much of myself, either.

Joseph was picking up his books when he heard the rattle of drums. He peered down the street and saw a group of Union soldiers marching toward him. Their flag rippled in the breeze, and the sight of it filled him with pride. *How can Franz even think of fighting against the Stars and Stripes? And how could I hide my loyalty to it— and to all it represents?*

Dimly aware of the ringing of the school bell, he stood at attention, his hand over his heart, until the flag passed. It wasn't until he started toward the building that Joseph realized he wasn't alone—Charles was waiting for him. They hurried up the stairs together, and Charles said, "I thought I was the only Unionist here. It sure is good to find out I'm not."

"And I'm glad to find out I'm not the only one who kept my Unionist sympathies to myself," Joseph said, holding the door for his classmate. "I'm a scholarship student, incidentally," he said as they walked down the deserted hallway. "My family lives near the harbor." *There. Now I don't have to worry that he might find out.*

Charles said, "We live uptown. My friends call me Charlie, by the way."

Joseph barely hesitated before he said, "At home I'm called Yosef, because my parents are from Germany, but I go by Joseph here at school."

How Much of This Book Is True?

Joseph and the other characters are all imaginary, but some of the people mentioned in the story are real, including Mayor Brown, General Butler, and Ross Winans (the elderly legislator who was imprisoned "for being a secessionist"). There are scores of firsthand—and sometimes conflicting—accounts of the unrest in Baltimore at the start of the Civil War, and I used details from many of them in this story, keeping in mind what it would be reasonable for Joseph to have witnessed and understood. I made up most of the bulletins he read at the newspaper office as well as most of the newspaper headlines, but the news itself is accurate—and people really did crowd around the bulletin boards at newspaper and telegraph offices.

What Happened Next?

As soon as Baltimore was subdued and the state's secession was no longer an immediate threat, the Federal government turned its attention across the Potomac to Confederate Virginia. A buffer zone must be created to protect the capital, and the city of Alexandria, not far downstream, must be occupied in order to keep the river open to shipping.

Meanwhile, in Baltimore, military officials issued a proclamation forbidding any conduct disloyal to the Federal government. This included wearing red and white—the colors of the secessionist cockade, or badge, and of the flag carried by Maryland soldiers fighting on the Confederate side. And when the poem "My Maryland," which urged that the state secede, was set to music as "Maryland, My Maryland," the song was banned.

Because Lincoln had suspended the writ of habeas corpus—the Constitutional right to protection from illegal imprisonment—people were jailed at Fort McHenry simply because of their southern sympathies. Ordinary citizens as well as Baltimore's mayor, its police chief, and two newspaper editors were among those imprisoned without a trial in 1861. Thirty-one Maryland state legislators were also arrested.

Union soldiers continued to garrison Fort McHenry and remained on Federal Hill throughout the war. They established numerous other forts and camps in and around the city, too.

The rest of Maryland came under Union military control, as well. This was partly to guard the boundary with Virginia, partly to protect the B&O Railroad and the C&O Canal, and partly to guarantee that Maryland stayed in the Union. There was still concern that the state would secede and leave Washington surrounded by enemy territory and isolated from the loyal states.

Though the Federal military presence was especially strong near the Potomac River fords, like Joseph's brother Franz, thousands of Maryland men crossed the Potomac into Virginia to join the Confederate army. About a fourth of Maryland's Civil War soldiers fought for the South.

ABOUT THE COVER PICTURE

This is one of many contemporary images representing the riot in Baltimore, an event that captured the nation's attention because it resulted in the first casualties of the growing conflict. (There had been no deaths on either side during the bombardment of Fort Sumter.)

Because the Pratt Street Riot, as it is often called, took place on the anniversary of the Battle of Lexington, the first battle of the American Revolution, this picture was titled "The Lexington of 1861."

LOOK FOR BOOK 1 IN THIS TRILOGY—

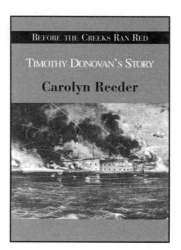

BEFORE THE CREEKS RAN RED

TIMOTHY DONOVAN'S STORY

Carolyn Reeder

AMERICA ON THE BRINK OF CIVIL WAR!

LOOK FOR BOOK 3
IN THIS TRILOGY—

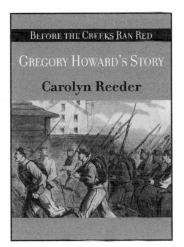

WAR COMES TO VIRGINIA!
(available in Spring '08)

ABOUT THE AUTHOR

Carolyn Reeder writes for young people because she knows from her experience as a classroom teacher that "kids love a good story." She writes historical fiction because she likes the challenge and enjoys the research. "You see," she explains, "research is my excuse to read about fascinating events, to talk to people I wouldn't otherwise meet, to go places I haven't been before—and to call it 'work.'"

To find out more about the author and her books, visit www.reederbooks.com.